D0483439

Up From
Jericho Tel

Up From Jericho Tel

by
E. L. Konigsburg

A YEARLING BOOK

Published by
Dell Publishing Co., Inc.
1 Dag Hammarskjold Plaza
New York, New York 10017

Yearling ® TM 913705, Dell Publishing Co., Inc.

ISBN: 0-440-49142-8

Reprinted by arrangement with Macmillan Publishing Company
on behalf of Atheneum Publishers.

Printed in the United States of America

September 1987

10 9 8 7 6 5 4 3 2 1

CW

For ROBERT, LESLEY and TERRY —
The Generation Received, full grown and
in full flower — with love

Up From
Jericho Tel

one

THERE WAS a time when I was eleven years old—between the start of a new school year and Midwinter's Night—when I was invisible. I was never invisible for long, and I always returned to plain sight, but all my life has been affected by the people I met and the time I spent in a world where I could see and not be seen.

It happened not so long ago, less than a year after Congress had passed the anti-hijacking bill. The airlines had not yet put in X-ray equipment, so the checking had to be done by hand. My mother had trained to become an airport security guard; she had learned what to search for in the suitcases and pocketbooks that passengers carried on board. She proved to be quick and thorough at it, so she got a job at one of the world's busiest airports, Kennedy International, serving the New York metropolitan area.

Late that August we hauled our trailer from Texas to Long Island, way out on the island, beyond the highways and before the Hamptons, to where there were duck farms and fields of potatoes and cabbages. To the Empire Estates Mobile Homes Park. We arrived in time for the beginning of the school year.

After three weeks at Singer Grove Middle School, I still ate lunch by myself. After three weeks, no one but my teachers called me Jeanmarie. I was nameless and furious. Furious at being nameless. Furious that no one recognized that I was a future famous person. Furious at having moved seventeen hundred miles only to find that the in-crowd were clones of the cheerleaders and jocks that I had gone to school with in Texas. Clones: lived in houses not mobile homes; had two parents, the mothers of which made cakes for PTA bake sales; talked to each other on the phone for hours; had been friends with each other since the world began. Clones were never alone.

IT ALL STARTED with a dead blue jay.

I had a tendency toward carsickness that I did not choose to demonstrate or discuss, so I always scrambled to claim a bus seat just behind the driver, where the exhaust fumes did not smell as bad and the bus did not pitch and roll as much. I was always the first one off the bus at my stop, and I always started home the minute my feet hit the ground, looking down, not looking back. So I was well ahead of everyone else when I saw the bird and stopped.

There was no blood showing, and it looked more stunned

4

than dead. I bent down to see if I could detect at least a little flutter. I had no intention of touching it; birds could carry a dread disease called parrot fever. Never mind that this was not a parrot. I did not want to die before I became famous. I was bending over, trying not to inhale any of the air between the bird and me, when Malcolm Soo caught up with me and stopped to see what had made me stop.

"I wonder if it's really dead," I said. "It may have flown into a window and gotten stunned."

Malcolm got down on his knees and put his face heroically close to the bird's beak, then leaned back and with his bare hand gently turned the bird over. "Dead," he said.

I swallowed hard, hoping to dissolve any bad air I may have consumed. I managed to say, "We ought to keep it from rotting."

"Everything rots," Malcolm replied.

"It ought to be buried," I said.

"It will still rot. It will just rot out of sight."

I didn't think a person had to see every bad thing that happened, and I also didn't think I had to discuss the fact that I didn't believe it. Death and dying were heavy items among the clones at Singer Grove Middle School. I avoided those discussions. I developed symptoms of any long, mysterious, illnesses that the clones cared to talk about. It seemed to me that every tragic illness started out like a common cold, and only after the disease was beyond cure did it produce the lumps and running sores that killed you. I saw my body as an incubator for thousands of viruses, all of them waiting for one wrong breath to enter and attack and kill me before I had a chance to show the world and its clones what I was really made of. Our teacher last year had shown us a

5

film strip of microscopic life in a drop of water, and I thought that it should have had an R rating; I found the unseen world violent, full of sex and with no redeeming social value.

"Do you want to help bury the bird?" I asked Malcolm, hoping that he would take over the job entirely. I didn't want to pick it up, and I surely didn't want it to remain above ground where it would reek and rot—since everything does—and infest all of the Empire Estates with parrot fever.

Malcolm took his map of the states west of the Mississippi—it was the largest and heaviest piece of paper he had—and slid it under the jay. "I think we ought to," he said.

I agreed. We decided to go home, deposit our books and meet to perform a burial service. Malcolm pinched the two ends of his map together, making a hammock for the dead bird to ride in as we walked the rest of the way.

"That was a nice map," I said, "very neat." I had had the same assignment, but my map had a red palm print on the northwest corner of Arizona where I had dragged my hand across wet paint because I had forgotten to work from north to south, and I had left the second *o* out of Colorado and had had to add it with a caret. My map was accurate but not worth putting on the refrigerator door.

"I'm very neat," Malcolm said. "It's a talent I have."

"Being neat is just something that is easier for some people than for others."

"That's why I would call it a talent," Malcolm said. "Like playing the piano is easier for some people than it is for others, and that's called a talent."

I told him that I would call it congenital, like a heart murmur or a strawberry birthmark or a clubfoot.

"If someone has an ability that they are born with—whether they develop it or not—that ability is called a talent. Take gymnastics . . ."

I said, "A person can be born with a hare lip and not inherit it. Hare lips are congenital."

"I never heard of a newborn with a hairy lip."

"Hare lip. H-A-R-E lip. It's congenital."

"Neatness is a talent. My father is neat. I am neat . . ."

"Listen, Malcolm, I wouldn't mind hearing you list your talents and virtues except that I think that it might start to stink before you finish," I said, looking at the bird. I was finding it difficult to talk without breathing in.

We arranged to meet at the spot where we were standing.

Malcolm and I were both latchkey children. I had noticed that he was the very first day of school. (Clones were never latchkeys.) Malcolm's father worked in the duck processing plant on the edge of town. His father's business was almost as seasonal as my mother's, for ducks and travel were both popular during the holidays. My mother had been told that during the peak travel seasons she would sometimes have to work the evening shift as well as every other weekend.

I wore a housekey on a metal chain around my neck, under my blouse. I had lost four keys during the first six weeks of school last year before Mother came up with the idea of my wearing my key around my neck. Malcolm never lost a key. Malcolm always knew exactly where his was. He didn't even take his key ring out of his side pocket until he was at his trailer's door. Key losing is congenital.

I dumped my books on the sofa and began looking for the trowel we had used when Mother and I had tried to grow tomatoes outside our trailer in Texas. The plants had grown about a foot high when huge caterpillars attacked. They were covered with hundreds of tiny white cocoons, and if you picked them off and stepped on them, they squished out the most disgusting green stuff. I decided that it was punishment enough for them to have to go through life looking as ugly as they did, so I left them alone, and they ate up all the tomato plants. We had no harvest at all.

I couldn't find the trowel.

I took a soup spoon from one of the kitchen drawers and started out the door when I had a second thought and returned. I rummaged through the closet in my room until I found a bottle of ink and a calligraphy pen that Mother's (boy)friend had given me last Christmas. I had liked the idea of doing calligraphy, but I could not get the hang of it. It was not easy to hold the pen at the proper angle so that both the up-and-down and the crosswise stroke of the + sign were the same thickness. If I concentrated on how I wrote, what I wrote made no sense at all. Besides, I always managed to get enough fingerprints on the paper so that it looked more like an FBI file than a page of beautiful handwriting. I suspected that even if Malcolm Soo could not do calligraphy, he was congenitally neat enough to do a weathergram.

A weathergram is what I wanted for the dead blue jay.

I took a brown grocery bag from Mother's supply and put the spoon, the bottle of ink and the pen into the bag and ran out to meet Malcolm. I guessed that he would have a proper digging tool and that even if it wasn't new, it would look new.

He did. It did.

We decided to bury the jay as far away from civilization as

we could; and since both of us had strict orders not to leave the grounds of The Empire Estates Mobile Homes Park, we walked to the part of it that had not yet been cleared for trailer hook-ups. We weaved our way through a stand of evergreens where the underbrush was ragged and full of sticklers until we found ourselves in a clearing. As we stood in its center, we saw that the pines that we had been walking through were part of a thick protecting circle that marked the clearing off, not only from the settled part of the trailer park but also from the part that had never been cleared. Except for a narrow opening on the far side of the trailer park, the circle was complete. It was not a large space, only about as big as a two-sofa family room in the home of the average clone. It was comfortably large and comfortably small.

We knew as soon as we saw it that it was the proper place to bury the jay. Together we pushed aside a mattress of pine needles and dug a grave, and Malcolm placed the jay, wrapped in The States West of the Mississippi, into it. He gathered up some pine cones and made a small pyramid of them. "This will be the grave marker. Not a gravestone but a gravecone."

"Clever, but not too clever," I said.

Malcolm said that it didn't seem right to bury the bird without saying something.

It was then that I reached into the grocery bag and brought out the calligraphy pen and the ink. I tore a strip of paper from the bag and handed it to Malcolm. "It's biodegradable," I said. "We'll do a weathergram." I told him that a weathergram is a poem of ten words or less that a person writes on plain brown paper and hangs on a tree.

"Why would a person do that?" he asked.

"Because that's the way a person delivers a weathergram," I told him. "The message is rubbed by the wind, faded by the sun, washed by the rain and becomes part of the world."

He shrugged his shoulders. "I get the idea," he said. "You sure have a talent for the dramatic."

I almost told him then that I was a future star of stage, screen and TV, but I didn't. At the moment I thought that Malcolm Soo could wait with the clones and the rest of the world to find out, but his remark made me gentle. "I'm sure you are a neat writer," I said kindly, "so I want you to write: *May your soul have flown to Heaven before you sank to Earth.*"

"It doesn't rhyme."

"It doesn't have to."

"It's more than ten words. It's twelve," he said, counting on his fingers.

"Write it," I said.

Malcolm wrote.

"And be sure to capitalize both Heaven and Earth."

Malcolm finished and held up the strip of paper, pleased with it and himself. I examined it and said, "You're neat all right, Malcolm, but you are not perfect. It should be s-o-u-l, not s-o-l-e. I don't know for sure if birds have s-o-u-l-s but I know for sure that they don't have s-o-l-e-s."

"Is a crow a bird?" Malcolm asked.

"Of course it's a bird."

"Then how come when people get old, they say that they get crow's feet around their eyes?"

"That's an expression."

"Is a duck a bird?"

I nodded.

"Then how come when someone's feet point out when they walk, they say that they are duckfooted?"

"That's another expression."

"Is a pigeon a bird?"

I said. "I know what you're going to say. You're going to tell me that when someone toes in, they say that he's pigeon-toed."

"I have just one more thing to ask you."

"What's that?"

"If they have feet, then how come they don't have soles?"

"Because they don't. Horses have feet and they have hooves, and dogs have feet and they have paws, and birds have feet, but they don't have soles. Trust me, Malcolm. You can have feet and not have a sole."

"How do you know that birds have s-o-u-l-s?"

"How do you know that they don't?"

Malcolm rewrote the weathergram. He did an even better job the second time than the first, which surprised me because when I tried to improve an artistic effort, it never came out neater or better the second time. Malcolm's letters were distinct and clear, every ascender was firm and complete, every descender was looped if it was meant to be, and every *t* had its cross. Malcolm was pleased with the way the weathergram looked, and I thought that what it said was worthy of a Hallmark.

Together we walked to the center tree of the inside row of the circle. It was a pine that stood slightly out of line with the others; it seemed to be asking us to hang our weathergram there, and we did. When we stood back, the strip of brown paper was ruffled by a slight breeze that came up, and I had the distinct feeling that our message was on its way.

Together we walked to the middle of the clearing and stood on either side of the small grave and listened. There were no sounds of traffic from the road. There was only the late afternoon sound of small animals and insects; it was an uneven hum, pitched low and restful. There were no manufactured smells: no gasoline or asphalt or insect repellent. There was the quiet odor of the pines and the sweet smell of leaves at rest after a summer's work. I wanted to take deep breaths so that I could fill up with all the wonderful smells at once. I looked around and could not find a single reminder of Empire Estates. There was nothing to tell us what day of the week it was or what year. There was nothing there to tell us that it was the twentieth century; even the fading afternoon light could have been dawn as easily as dusk.

As we walked out of the circle of trees, I felt as if I were taking out more than I had brought in, even though we were leaving the weathergram and the buried jay behind. I walked out of there with a feeling of closeness to Malcolm that I had not had when we had gone in. I said to him, "Next time, we can circle around and enter from that opening on the far side instead of weaving our way through the trees. That way it will feel more like an amphitheater," and when Malcolm nodded his agreement, I knew that we had made a promise that there would be a next time.

THE VERY NEXT DAY we found a luna moth. "I'll get my spoon," I said the minute I spotted it.

"And the stuff for its weathergram," Malcolm added as he reached down and picked the moth up by the tip of its body and held it so that no dust would rub away from its eerily beautiful wings.

I was pleased that Malcolm wanted another weathergram, and I thought that I composed an award winner, *Fly. Flutter. Falter. Fall*, but Malcolm again complained that it didn't rhyme, and I said that only a person who was neat to the point of being sick would need poems that did. I told Malcolm that he made the *F*'s so beautiful that I thought that they might alight from the paper and leave the weathergram on wings of their own. "I have excellent small muscle coordination," he said.

❦ ❦ ❦

WE BEGAN walking to and from the bus stop together, studying the ground to find candidates for a funeral service. Nothing turned up on either Thursday or Friday, and on the following Monday just when we reached the steps of my trailer, Malcolm said that he would see me at the burial ground, and I said sure, and we gave up pretending that we needed to bury something to spend time together.

Malcolm Soo had been born in Korea but didn't remember the language. He was a half-orphan. He had gone to Milton Road Elementary before Singer Grove, which meant that he knew one-third of the sixth grade clones, but he hardly paid any attention to them. He didn't even realize they were clones. Malcolm Soo was five weeks younger than me but just as bossy. He also considered himself a future famous person, but, unlike me, he was perfectly willing to talk about it. He had decided that he would win a Nobel Prize in science. He had not yet decided whether he would win it in chemistry or physics, but whatever he discovered, he would name after his dear dead mother, Chin-i. He was neat, methodical and had an opinion about everything. I was not neat, not methodical and had an opinion about everybody. He had opinions about things I had never even thought about. I had opinions of people he had never even noticed. I did not find Malcolm Soo as boring as afternoon television. I did not find him boring at all.

$$ \maltese \ \maltese \ \maltese $$

MALCOLM was alone when he found the next victim. He carried it over to my place and knocked on my door. "We need another funeral," he said. He ceremoniously unwrapped the neat folds of the aluminum foil (broiler-strength) package and showed me what I thought was a black caterpillar with a glandular problem. "A mole," he said.

We walked to the clearing on the edge of the Park and dug a grave. Malcolm took up the pen and asked me what the mole's epigraph was to be.

"Write *That was light at the end of the tunnel. Sorry.* Put two *n*'s in *tunnel*, and remember to put the *e* before the *l*."

"I know a tunnel when I see one," Malcolm said.

"I have no doubt that you would know one when you see one. I'm not sure you could spell one."

"O-n-e," Malcolm said.

14

"No one likes a smartass, Malcolm," I replied.

"It takes one to know one."

We hung the weathergram from the same tree that held the other two. "Imagine living your whole life underground," Malcolm said. "Imagine finding the light at the end of the tunnel, and then, zap! you're dead."

"I don't expect to let that happen to me," I told him. "I want to be like the luna moth. I want to fly before I fall."

"But the moth also lives in the dark."

"And so do the stars," I said.

"I like the stars," he said. "I like astronomy. I'd like to discover a star some day."

"Good. Then I'll let you discover me."

"What kind of star do you want to be?"

I had never told anyone that I wanted to be a great actress. No one in Texas. Not even my mother. And yet that wanting took up most of my dream life. I had never told anyone and had never done anything about it. I had never even tried out for the Fifth Grade Christmas Pageant. It was as if trying for it would show everyone some secret, hidden part of myself that they could make fun of and hurt.

Since the day when we had buried the blue jay, I knew that I would tell Malcolm. I knew that I could trust him. Friendships and funerals may begin on common ground, but they have to go deeper. Friendships and funerals both require faith. Faith is a kind of bond, a kind of trust. I knew that Malcolm would not make fun of me if I told him my secret. And he would never tell anyone; I wouldn't even have to ask him not to.

So I told Malcolm Soo that I dreamed of becoming an

15

actress. I told him that I wanted to be a great one, one they would name theaters after.

"You may not be pretty enough, but you sure are peculiar enough."

"Great actresses don't have to be beautiful; it's more important to make people think you're beautiful than to be beautiful. I told you I want them to name *theaters*, not hairstyles, after me. What do you want to have named after you?"

"A planet, an atomic particle and ten bastard sons."

"That's disgusting."

Malcolm laughed. "What have you done about becoming an actress?"

"Telling you is the first thing."

❦ ❦ ❦

I THOUGHT that we ought to give the burial place a name. Malcolm suggested Pet Cemetery, but I complained that the name was ordinary and besides none of the animals we had buried had been pets. "I'll think of what to call it," I said. I knew that something would come to me, something that was as appropriate as Coca-Cola and as dignified as IBM. There was a name buzzing in the back of my head, and one day when we were just sitting there, a day when we weren't burying anything, just holding our heads up to the sun to catch some rays, I heard a voice saying, "Jericho Tel" and was surprised to recognize the voice as my very own.

"We'll call this place Jericho Tel," I repeated.

Malcolm liked the sound of it. Jericho Tel seemed right to him, too, even though at the time I couldn't tell him what it meant. There was no logic to the name, but it seemed right, and the fact that it seemed right without reason to Malcolm made me all the more certain that it was.

When I got home, I looked up Jericho Tel. Jericho was the oldest inhabited city in the world. Tel meant hill. But the land in our clearing was flat. I wondered if the clearing was the top of a buried hill. Could we be standing on top of something that lay deep, deep under us? Something as old as civilization. I was excited by that thought.

❦ ❦ ❦

THE BABY SQUIRREL that had fallen from its nest was next, and when we buried it, I composed, and Malcolm wrote the following weathergram: *By dying young, you have missed a lot of nuts.*

Malcolm complained that not only did that poem not rhyme, it was the most non-poetic poem he had ever heard. I did not have a high opinion of it either, but I said, "The word count is accurate. Write it anyway." And Malcolm wrote.

When we hung the squirrel's weathergram from the tree, I noticed that our first one, the blue jay's, was only a tatter, and all the letters had faded away. Our first message had been delivered. I didn't say anything to Malcolm. He would want to know who had gotten the message, and I wouldn't be able to tell him. I didn't want to defend without proof something that I knew as certainly as I knew that.

Tallulah says, *"Exercise is good for the heart, the lungs and the unemployed."*

two

Two DAYS LATER we found the dog. It was a Dalmatian, and it was lying near the edge of Jericho Tel. It was the most pitiful looking of all the creatures that we had found, not only because it was the largest and not only because it had died with its eyes open but also because there was something majestic about it.

"I'll bet it's purebred," I said.

Malcolm leaned over the corpse and studied it. It was the first time I had thought of one of our dead creatures as being a corpse. "This dog belonged to someone," he said. He motioned for me to come join his inspection. I stood by the side of the dog but did not bend over. Malcolm pointed, "Look where the fur around the neck is worn. That's where she wore a collar. I think someone killed her and threw the collar

18

away so the dog couldn't be identified. There's no drag marks, so they probably dumped her here."

"Him," I said.

Malcolm looked. "Him," he said.

Besides not liking the idea that someone had murdered a dog and dumped it, I did not like the idea that someone else knew about Jericho Tel. "I guess a soup spoon won't do this job," I said.

"Of course not," Malcolm said. "We'll need shovels."

"I don't have a shovel."

"We keep one in our storage room. You probably do, too."

"I don't know how to get into ours."

"The same key that opens your trailer opens your storage."

"You're a great detail man, Malcolm."

"It's another one of my talents."

We walked to the far corner of Empire Estates where the storage lockers were located. Malcolm told me that they were numbered the same way as the lot numbers, and I told him that I had a sufficiently logical mind to have figured that out. I found storage room A-10. I didn't want to go inside. The air stuck to you like jelly. I may not have been a neat person, but I can say that I hated having dirty hands more than any one who was. I found the shovel, tied together with a rake and a grass edger, standing in the corner next to Mother's wedding dress sealed in a Keepsake Box. Everything in that storage room was as dusty and as useful as the wedding dress in the Keepsake Box. The shovel was rusty. I hated touching rusty things. They could give you lockjaw. Lockjaw started with the symptoms of the common cold.

The tools were tied together with a length of old rope.

I could not loosen the knot, and I had nothing to cut it with, so I stood there in the hot windowless space and tried pushing the loose ends of the rope up through the knot, getting hotter and more resentful of the Dalmatian for dying on our Jericho Tel. I knew that I was going to rot before the Dalmatian, and I kicked the shovel and hurt my toe and screamed and swore.

Malcolm heard and headed in my direction.

He stood by the storage room door and asked, "Can I be of assistance?"

"Isn't it obvious that you can. Do you have a knife to cut this stupid rope?"

He walked to the corner where I was wrestling with the rope and picked up the whole packet of tools and lay them down flat on the floor. He then pulled the shovel out lengthwise as I watched. He handed me the shovel.

"Let's get going," I said.

"If you had done that for me, I would have said thank you."

"You probably would have," I replied. "I don't have a talent for good manners."

"Good manners are training, not talent."

"Listen, Malcolm, I'm not anybody's trained monkey, and I probably have gotten brown lung disease from all the dust in here." I marched in front of him toward the door. He didn't move. "I'm locking this place up," I said. Malcolm stormed out, saying nothing.

By the time we reached Jericho Tel, the silence between us had become so hostile that I started thinking of nice things to say to break it, and I would have said the one nice thing I had thought of if, after we got to the center of the

Tel, he had not put his shovel down and said, "That's some kind of mouth you have," so instead of saying something nice, I said, "It's congenital."

"I've got to be some kind of wonderful to put up with it."

"Being wonderful must be congenital," I said. Our argument could have grown to a full-scale fight if at that moment I had not caught sight of the dead dog and said, "I hate to bury him naked."

Malcolm said, "I'll start digging while you go home and get a plastic garbage bag."

"A garbage bag! You can't treat a dead Dalmatian like garbage!"

"Okay. I'll start digging while you go home and get a plastic burial shroud."

"Where will you start?"

"Dead center," he said.

"Very funny."

"I'm serious. You pace it off in one direction. I'll pace it off in the other, and we'll meet dead center."

So we did. Malcolm counted the number of steps of one diameter, and I the other, and then we met halfway. Malcolm pushed aside the thin layer of pine needles and scuffed the dirt making an X with his foot. He told me that he would start digging there, and I started home to get the plastic shroud.

I was walking back toward Jericho Tel when the sky changed. It was the time of year when the air was announcing a change of seasons, and the sky seemed too weak to hold any heat a minute past sundown. But suddenly the sky changed from blue to a combination of lilac and green, and the clouds became caramel-colored. It was a stained glass sky; parts of it seemed unwilling to let light through. I peeked through the trees and saw the Dalmatian lying on its side and saw Malcolm push the edge of his shovel into the ground with his foot. I had glanced away for only a second, when I heard "H-E-L-L-L-L-P" and saw Malcolm disappearing into a hole in the ground.

I threw the garbage bag down and raced around to the opening in the circle of trees. I was barely at the edge when I felt myself being pulled into its center—where X had marked the spot—and before I could say or do anything, I was sucked down into the hole that Malcolm had dug.

Malcolm had hit a sinkhole or an old elevator shaft, I thought. There was a logical explanation for what was happening, and I would only have to wait to hear it from Malcolm. He would have a logical explanation. The trouble with logical explanations was that they only *made* sense. They never explained *senses*. And at the moment, when I should have been feeling frightened at being sucked down off the face of the earth, I was not. I was feeling calm, watching myself, listening to my thoughts and allowing myself to enjoy this swimming/floating/pulling feeling; it seemed safer than picking up rusty shovels. It seemed a perfect way for things to happen. I had always known that Jericho Tel had a logic all its own.

The force pulling me down stopped suddenly, and I was sitting on top of a lavender-colored metal box. The top was covered with what looked like the lead points of thousands of sharpened pencils pointing outward. None pricked. I didn't expect them to. I was deep in a hole, but I could see everything clearly. The light was not natural; it was as bright as our cafetorium except it did not have the harsh

22

look that comes from a ceiling full of fluorescent lightbulbs. Neither was it like the light that comes from the sun. It was soft, rosy and blond—a blend of the whispered colors of the rainbow: rose, not red; mauve not purple; aqua, apricot and lavender, all dusted with gold.

I began crawling over the surface of the box looking for a trapdoor, for my powers of reason had begun to work, and I thought that since Malcolm and his shovel had not greeted me at the bottom of the hole, he must have fallen inside the lavender box. He must have hit the latch on its trapdoor. A trapdoor on a lavender box seemed as logical as a lavender box itself, so I began tapping the surface with my elbow or knee, but not in any systematic way.

Just when I thought I had probably covered every square inch of the box—my elbow was feeling tender—I decided to rest. I did not panic. I did not even hurry. I simply sat on the box with my feet stretched before me and rested my head in my hands. I thought that I ought to try to think what Malcolm had done. Had he pounded on the lid? Had he jumped up and down? Had he tried to climb out? No. He had disappeared more easily than that. There had not been enough time between my seeing him being sucked into the hole and my arriving at the scene for him to have done anything.

So I sat on the top of the lavender box and waited. I examined my fingernails under the mysterious light; they seemed to glow with a soft blue light like a television screen that has just been turned off. If I looked up, I didn't see the sky. I saw an endless shaft filled with the same pastel golden glow. I did a quick check of my pulse and found that it was normal. I felt my armpits for sweat: none; my forehead for fever: none. I waited, pleased with my patience and my calm.

I stood up, and without warning I felt myself falling, falling, falling, feeling the way the astronauts look when they walked in space. It was a pleasant feeling, except for my stomach, which seemed to want to stay put while the rest of me twirled. Then with a fast triple spin, I landed feet up. Before I could get my eyes to focus or my bowels to settle, I heard a female voice, deep with impatience say, "Close the door before you let all that disgusting fresh air in."

I did as I was told and then walked forward into a room bathed in the same amber-rose light that had filled the shaft. The room was no larger than Jericho Tel itself, and sitting on an enormous sofa piled high with satin pillows in every pastel shade you could think of was a tall, slender woman with long straight red hair—a red that was as natural as lipstick—and a big red mouth (also as natural as lipstick). Her eyes were outlined in black pencil in addition to wearing such heavy false eyelashes that they looked as if she had glued a millipede over each. Her eyes were green and had that same shimmering look as the lavender beads on the box. Her fingernails were half the length of her fingers and were the same firecracker red as her mouth. She was wearing blue satin pajamas and was smoking a cigarette that she held in a long, black cigarette holder. That and her eyelashes were the only streaks of black in the soft glitter of the room.

Malcolm was standing at one end of the long sofa, leaning on his shovel.

"This is Tallulah," he said.

"Pleased to meet you," I said, extending my hand.

"She doesn't shake hands."

Tallulah took a long drag from her cigarette and blew out the smoke. Malcolm waved his hand in front of his face. "You'll get used to it," Tallulah said. She took another puff of her cigarette and blew the smoke into the space between Malcolm and me. "Being invisible will make your assignments easy, darlings."

"Are we invisible?" I asked.

"Not yet. You have to go through the Orgone." She lifted her eyes to the ceiling so that her eyelashes rested against her eye sockets like two small furry animals that Malcolm and I might have buried.

"Assignment?" Malcolm asked. "Assignment? How can you talk about an assignment when I haven't yet found out what I am doing here or how I got here or even what I am."

"What you are is an amateur, darling."

"Less than an hour ago, I was a kid . . ."

"Kids are amateur adults," Tallulah said.

"But . . ." Malcolm began protesting.

"Shut up, Malcolm," I said. "Let's listen to the woman."

Tallulah smiled and nodded. "Your first assignment is Carl A. Vogel," she said. "Exit upstage left. That should take you straight through the Orgone."

I started to leave, but Malcolm held back. "What are we supposed to do about Carl A. Vogel?"

Tallulah lowered her lashes and looked at Malcolm through hooded eyes. "You'll know what to do when you see him."

"How am I supposed to know that I *have* seen him. I've never laid eyes on Carl A. Vogel."

"Lucky," she said lighting a fresh cigarette from her old one. She delicately put the butt into a silver ashtray, as large

25

as a birdbath, that rested on a mother-of-pearl table near her elbow.

"I've had nightmares better than this," Malcolm said. "I have one nightmare where I am sitting in a classroom about to take a math exam, and I haven't opened the book all year. That nightmare is better than this assignment."

Tallulah said, "That's strange. I used to have that nightmare, too. I always thought it was because I never *had* opened the book all year. Math," she said making a face that turned everything in her face downward.

"I happen to like math very much, and I happen to be very good at it. It is one of my talents."

Tallulah took a deep puff of smoke and blew it out before turning to Malcolm to say, "Mathematics is for the dentists of the soul."

"If it weren't for mathematics, you wouldn't have computers."

"No, darling," Tallulah said, "*you* wouldn't. I never wanted one. I once had to learn how to operate an electric toaster, but I really didn't care for the work. There was no controlling the rye bread, and I never could get the bagels to fit into those narrow slots. Tallulah always burned her fingers pulling them out, and the one time she tried to get them out with a fork, she caused the lights to go out for five city blocks."

"About Carl A. Vogel. Can you give us a hint about how we are to do this assignment," Malcolm asked.

"Very well."

Malcolm moved closer to her, clearing the air in front of him by waving his hand. Tallulah continued looking at him. "Well," he said. "What is it?"

"What is what?"

"I asked you to give us a hint about how we are to do this assignment, and you said 'very well.' I'm waiting."

"That's how you're supposed to do it: very well. I want you to get these preliminaries over with so that you can find my necklace."

"What necklace?" I asked.

"My necklace containing The Regina Stone. It is simply beautiful, darlings. It was given to me by a fan in honor of my most famous role. As long as she wore it, Tallulah had good fortune." She looked into the distance and let the cigarette in the holder burn down. "Run along now. Upstage left and through the Orgone. Mr. Carl A. Vogel is your assignment."

We started out, but Tallulah called us back. "Left is right onstage, darlings. Upstage is back, and downstage is front. In the theater, darlings, the stage makes the world a mirror image. And remember, you are players now." As we started to leave again, she called out to us, "Bring me a pack of cigarettes, darlings. Herbert Tareyton is my brand. I like them king size and mentholated with filter tips."

"You really ought not to smoke," Malcolm said.

"Don't worry, darling. It won't kill me." She tilted her head back and laughed. "King size," she said, settling back into her bank of pillows. "Surely, someone up there must still smoke. The way they pick on smokers is enough to make me glad I left the real world when I did. Back of the bus. Back of the plane. Move your seat in a restaurant. The whole United States is becoming a health spa. Sometimes I get such a migraine from the pounding of the joggers' feet that I want to dig the ground out from under them, but they would be back within a week, pounding, pounding, pounding. Do you want to know the best kept secret in the western world? It's this: Baryshnikov smokes. Now if you can find anyone who moves better than he does, you kidnap him and bring him to me." She put a fresh cigarette into her holder. "Oh! I almost forgot," she said, sitting bolt upright. "You must say something beautiful when you've finished, so I'll know to bring you back. How about *fettucini alfredo*. Yes. Say that."

"*Fettucini alfredo*? What kind of a password is that?" Malcolm asked. "Even Jeanmarie could think of something more beautiful than that to say."

Tallulah said, "Well, it must be something that doesn't come up in ordinary conversation." She rubbed her forehead for a minute. "I have it. Say *Papillon!* That's French for butterfly. In the Middle Ages, butterflies were thought to be symbols of the soul." Then she looked at Malcolm and said mischievously, "That's s-o-u-l, darling."

Tallulah says, "*Onstage, an actress must remember that right and left, down and up are the exact opposites of what they are to the audience; backstage, she must forget it.*"

three

WE EXITED as Tallulah had told us to and were stopped dead by a jolt of air that was like a sock in the stomach. We remained paralyzed for what seemed like several minutes—time and space are difficult to measure when things are happening for the first time—with our hands hanging limply by our sides. Then another jolt of air, as forceful and as sudden as the one that had stopped us, pushed us up from where we stood, and we were swept side by side and upright into a huge box that vibrated with a soft sound, like the surface hum of a buried high power cable. The box glowed with a straw-colored light that deepened to amber as we waited. Malcolm appeared as calm and patient as I felt.

Soon we began twirling, and except for the feeling of air moving across my face and the worried messages I was getting from my stomach, I would never have known that I was twirling, for it was happening to Malcolm at the same speed and at the same time. Since I was pretty sure that I was not yet invisible, I hoped I would not throw up. I didn't want to create a mess in the buttery golden light of the Orgone.

Before I had time to decide what I would do with the mess if I made one, I found myself sitting with Malcolm on the edge of a stage set up in the front of a large tent. Row after row of people were sitting, waiting for something to begin. There were men in their shirt sleeves and women in three-piece pants suits with elastic waistbands. People were shuffling their feet or clearing their throats in the way that audiences do when they have settled down but not settled into the program they came for.

No one noticed that we had arrived. Malcolm was as clear to me as the hand at the end of my arm, and I guessed that I was clear to Malcolm, but no one, no one at all, noticed that we had arrived uninvited at the gathering.

I looked at Malcolm, and he looked at me. Then he faced the audience and stuck out his tongue. Nothing happened. We smiled at each other. Malcolm faced the audience again and crossed his eyes. Nothing happened. Once again we looked at each other and smiled. Then he crossed his eyes and stuck out his tongue, and no one, no one except me, noticed. We sat there on the edge of the stage and beamed.

We were truly, absolutely there for all the world not to see.

I had never felt this way before. Of course, I had never been invisible before, but that was not the greatest difference I felt. This invisible person both was me and was not. This invisible Jeanmarie sat relaxed on the edge of the podium and studied the audience. How wonderful to see and not be seen. It was a feeling so new that I had to define it by what it was not. It was not . . . it was not . . . hurried, and it was not . . .worried. I felt that a small, tight ache between my eyes had gone away, an ache that I had had for so long that I didn't know I had had it until it had gone away.

So, I thought, I can dance naked across the stage if I want to, and no one except Malcolm will know. I can smile, frown, make faces, spit—maybe not spit—scratch, throw up—maybe not throw up—and no one will notice.

But I didn't want to waste my invisibility doing things like that. I wanted to do the job we were supposed to: Mr. Carl A. Vogel. Without that little worry knot between my eyes, I clearly saw that I would know what we were supposed to do, and I knew that Malcolm and I would do it very well.

I sat there for another minute feeling perfectly relaxed in front of this strange audience. After I said *strange audience* to myself, I realized that it *was* strange. Not rather strange, but very strange. In the front row alone, seven people had crutches and one had an aluminum walker like the one Mrs. Quinn used. It seemed that every seventh person was in a wheelchair, and as I continued to study them, I was able to spot other things: twelve hearing aids; six people with dark glasses and white canes.

I felt a tap on my shoulder: Malcolm.

"What is this?" he asked. He pointed to a huge banner in back of the podium. It said, JOG WITH GOD. "Is it some kind of Special Olympics?" he asked.

At that point, a man with crutches in the front row turned

to the woman with the aluminum walker and said to her, "That was very clever."

"What was?" she asked.

"What you called this: A Special Olympics."

"Yes," she said. "Yes. That was clever."

I realized then that we could be heard but not seen. I looked at Malcolm, and we both laughed. We reminded each other to be quiet by holding our fingers to our lips. That made us laugh more, and the people in the front row looked at each other and smiled, too. I was the first to jump down off the edge of the stage. Malcolm followed.

As we walked between the rows of chairs, we bumped the knees of the people that we walked in front of. Unlike at the movies, no one here seemed to mind. But what seemed peculiar was that no one seemed to find it peculiar that their knees were being jostled and jogged. Jogged by God? I wondered. I couldn't resist testing my invisibility. I blew on the back of a man's neck, and he swatted it as if an insect had crawled there. I ran my fingers through the hair of a woman whose hair was as stiff as dacron from hair spray. The woman's hands flew up to her head to rescue her hairdo, and as she started patting it in place, I started patting her hands. There was a soft slap, slap sound, and the man who was sitting to her left watched in fascination as the woman tried to save her hairdo. Finally, she lowered her arms and did nothing while her curls unrolled one by one, and then just as miraculously rolled right back up and were refastened in place.

"How do you do that?" the man sitting next to her finally asked.

"I think about it. It's what you call a mind set."

32

"Oh!" he said. "I've heard that evil only exists in the mind, but I never have heard that said about beauty."

"Well, it does," she said.

"Suppose so," he answered.

Malcolm saw a woman lighting a cigarette from a pack that looked like Herbert Tareyton's. He signaled to me that he was heading in that direction. I followed.

As he moved between the rows, he bumped a gentleman's elbow, and out of habit he said "Excuse me," and the gentleman, out of habit said, "That's all right," without looking around.

Oh! I loved being invisible.

The woman had finished lighting her cigarette; she had blown out the match and was looking around to see what she should do with it—there were no ashtrays—when Malcolm delicately picked the match out from between her fingers. The woman hardly paid attention. As she put the package of cigarettes back into her pocketbook, she began talking to the old woman sitting in the wheelchair next to her. The old woman's face was twisted to one side, and spit was drooling out of the down-turned side of her mouth. Her left eye was sealed shut; her left hand was turned inward and stayed clenched in her lap. She was wearing a cocka-mamie black hat that had slipped over her right eye. In the band of the hat were three blue jay feathers. I knew we were where we were supposed to be.

The woman who had lighted the cigarette spoke to the old lady in the wheelchair. She spoke very softly. If Malcolm and I had been visible, we would not have been able to stand close enough to hear what she was saying.

"Now remember, Mary Frances, you don't get to be cured

33

until after Uncle Henderson over on the other side of the room has had his sight to come back."

The old woman in the wheelchair answered without changing her position, "You told me that four times already. What you have not made clear is when I get my money."

"You'll git your money after the tent is good and empty. Carl and me expect a Academy Award performance for what you're charging."

Through her twisted face, the old woman managed to say, "Union wages, Mrs. Vogel. Union wages. I'm a professional."

Mrs. Vogel noticed that that old man with the crutches on the other side of the aisle was watching them, so she straightened Mary Frances's hat and patted her hand and said, "Soon, soon, Mother dear. It won't be long now." She threw her cigarette butt on the dirt floor of the tent and ground it out with her shoe. Her purse sat in her lap.

Malcolm was itching to get his hands on that purse. Just as he leaned over, ready to pick it up off her lap, Mrs. Vogel said out loud, "Just you wait, Mama. You will walk again." Malcolm jumped back as her voice boomed. She suddenly seemed to get excited to a tizzy; she smiled and began nodding her head as if she were answering yes to twenty rapid-fire questions, and she started repeating, "You will walk again, old Mama. You will walk again." After she said it about a zillion times, she stood up to her full height and hollered, "Pray, let the music start. It will be Mama who will jog with God tonight." She was shouting loud enough for everyone in the audience as well as those backstage to hear.

Mary Frances produced a drooling, crooked smile, and one

34

of her eyes rolled up as if it operated on a circuit that had nothing to do with the other.

The music did start, and from behind the back flaps of the tent, there appeared two women dressed in white satin gowns with star-spangled belts. They approached the microphone and sang two hymns. After finishing with the words of the second song, the two songstresses began humming. They hummed through the better part of a whole song before they began clapping their hands and chanting, "Reverend Carl, Reverend Carl, Reverend Carl," louder and louder and louder until the audience picked up on it and started chanting, "Reverend Carl," in huge swells of sound. By now the two songstresses were stamping their feet and snapping their fingers and wagging their heads enough to make their hair fray at the edges. Soon they backed further and further off stage until finally they retreated outside the back tent flaps.

The next thing that happened was that the lights went down, down, down, while the audience kept up the chant, "Reverend Carl, Reverend Carl . . ." The lights went out for a second and then came back on full force to show a man dressed all in white except for his necktie, which was a big blue bow. He was a tall, lean man. Up close you could see that he was wearing pancake makeup; it had gotten caught in his eyebrows and in his hairline and gave them a dusty peach look. He had the biggest set of false teeth I had ever seen. When he smiled—which he did often—his mouth looked like a piano keyboard with the sharps missing. He whistled the letter s. He lifted the microphone from its stand and said, "Brothers and Sisters, the time has come for us to talk together and walk together and jog with God."

Malcolm and I had moved to the front of the tent and stood just under the stage and listened while Reverend Carl E. Vogel told everyone that only the pure in heart were ready to jog with God, and if they were not pure in heart or were not sure if they were, he could lay his hands on them and make them pure and ready and able to jog with God. I noticed that the two songstresses had circled around the outside of the tent and reentered through the back. They stood to the rear of the audience.

Reverend Carl was saying, "There is no crippled body but that there is a crippled soul. Tonight, good people, we will stop the suffering, cure the crippled, heal the helpless. We will unleash the powers of good and imprison the forces of evil. Amen to you, I say. Come forward, the lame, the halt and the blind. Come forward unto me. I will have my assistants to move throughout this audience, and they will be happy to help to bring forward those of you who want the purifying touch of my hands upon your crippled souls." He paused and lowered his head and left it down for a good minute while the audience stayed so quiet that not even a cough was to be heard. He lifted his head slowly, as if it was a weight too great to bear. And maybe with those teeth it was. He said, "Come forward, come to me," he said softly as he held his hands outward in a beckoning gesture and closed his eyes.

And that is when Malcolm walked onstage and unzipped his fly.

The Reverend Carl felt himself becoming undone and looked down, which had the happy result of making everyone in the audience look, too. He turned his back to the audience and quickly zipped his pants and circled back, smiling saying, "Come unto me, I say," leaning forward and moving his arms in a gathering motion.

Malcolm struck again.

The Reverend Carl's smile melted faster than Jell-O in a microwave. He spun around and refastened his pants in such a hurry that he forgot that he was still holding the microphone, and everyone heard the sound of the zipper, magnified like—well, like the buzz of a fly.

Reverend Carl quickly turned to face his audience again, "Bring me your crippled souls, your crippled bodies. Bring them unto me so that . . ."

Malcolm, again.

The Reverend Carl was so distracted that he could not finish his sentence. He turned his back to the audience again and called, "Sister Booth and Sister Love, we need more of your songs. Come ye back to this platform, and let your voices sing forth the coming down the aisles of these broken bodies and souls." He zipped again and held his hands high, keeping his back to the audience and his eyes on his fly. Sisters Booth and Love must not have heard him or not believed him, for they were not forthcoming, and the Reverend made the plea once again, louder. "Sister Booth and Sister Love, will you please to get back up on this here stage now and sing us some songs."

One of the Sisters called from the back of the tent, "Will you be wantin' Sister Love to do the stage lights now, Reverend?"

"Ah, Sister Booth, step on up here and raise your voice in song in praise of our Lord."

Sister Booth said, "Sure thing, Rev." She put the brake on a wheelchair she was rolling forward and called across the rows, "Sister Love, honey, the Reverend wants you to make that nightly miracle of the lights, while I go on and give these here folks another of our Lord's marching songs."

Sister Booth stepped forward and took the microphone from Reverend Carl's hand and began to sing. Reverend Carl turned around and smiled at his audience, glanced down at the front of his trousers and then fastened his eyes on the man with crutches across the aisle from Mrs. Vogel and Mary Frances.

"Brother," he said, "Brother, if you have known pain, come on up here and let me help you to throw away those crutches and jog with God."

The man was not sure that the Reverend Carl had spoken to him. He pointed to himself, and the Reverend nodded. Then Mrs. Vogel stood up and called, "Reverend, Reverend Carl!"

"Yes, my dear," he said turning a saintly smile in her direction.

"Reverend, my mama here is in awful shape since her stroke four years ago this July. She ain't got too many more days, Reverend, and I would like for her to be able to jog on up to them Pearly Gates. Can we come forward, too?"

"Come," he said, "My arms are open . . ."

He should not have said open, for as soon as he did, Malcolm unzipped his pants again. This time Reverend Carl buttoned his jacket, pleased with himself for having thought of it. Malcolm unknotted the blue bow at his neck. Reverend Carl pulled it out from under his collar and threw it to Mrs. Vogel. "Come," he said, "with faith and with my healing hands, her body will become as unknotted as easily as I undo my scarf."

38

Mrs. Vogel hurriedly hung her pocketbook over the back of Mary Frances's wheelchair and pushed the old lady up to the front of the stage, bumping over feet and crutches in her hurry to get there. Reverend Carl knelt down at the edge of the stage, making welcoming motions with his hands until he noticed that he had opened up the split in his pants displaying blue drawers that matched his bow tie. He shot bolt upright and sang out, "Bring that sweet Mama of yours up here on stage, and we will witness the miracle of my healing hands."

Mrs. Vogel had to turn Mary Frances around and bump her up the steps backwards to get her onstage, and Mary Frances's cockamamie hat hung down near her right nostril, but she held onto her lopsided position and continued to drool as if she couldn't be any other way. Carl Vogel approached the wheelchair, and Mary Frances still looked as if she had been frozen in that position by some medical process that didn't deserve a good name. He raised his hands over her head and began to ask Mrs. Vogel questions such as: had she been a healthy, happy woman before she had been felled by this stroke. Mrs. Vogel brought tears to her eyes and assured Reverend Carl that her Mama was the healthiest, happiest person in Tompkins County and the two counties that bordered it.

Reverend Carl put his hands on top of Mary Frances's head and started mumbling, and Sister Booth called through the flap, "Hey, Sister Love, honey, cut them lights to major miracle size." And the lights went down.

Reverend Carl continued mumbling, mumbling, and then he lifted his eyes up and began praying out loud, looking at the ceiling of the tent the whole time. He spoke faster than any human being I had ever heard, but by listening carefully to what he said, I heard him asking for guidance, good weather and a winning ticket on the state lottery. He then brought his hands down and tapped Mary Frances's head and said, "Arise, little woman. We have given your pain to the Lord. You can walk now." He tapped her head again, but Mary Frances did not move.

Mrs. Vogel straightened the hat, and one of the blue jay feathers came off in her hand, and she began tearing at it as she said, "Mama, Reverend Carl says that you can walk now."

Mary Frances did not move.

Reverend Carl did some hocus-pocus with his hands and did some more chanting at the ceiling and then tapped her on the head again. "Arise, my child," he said.

Mary Frances did not move.

"Arise and jog." Reverend Carl said.

Mary Frances did not move.

"Get up!" Mrs. Vogel said. "For God's sake, Mama, get up."

I walked around to where Sister Booth was standing and wrestled the microphone out of her hand. I put my mouth right up to the microphone and breathed into it like an obscene telephone caller, and then I panted into it until the sounds seemed to invade every corner of the tent. Then, when I knew I had their attention, I said, "You told her not to be cured until after Uncle Henderson over on the other side of the room has his sight to come back."

And the next thing that happened was that Reverend Carl whispered to Mrs. Vogel, "Get Sister Love to cut them damn lights and git this dame out of here."

The lights did go off for a minute, but then they went on to their brightest and stayed on. I knew then that Malcolm had found the switch and was making certain that Mr. Carl Vogel would be shown in full light.

Reverend Carl was standing red-faced in front of Mary Frances's wheelchair, and Mrs. Vogel was wringing her hands behind it. I went over there and began to push Mary Frances across the stage and down the steps and out the back of the tent. The whole time the old actress did not change her warped look or stop drooling. For all the world it looked like the wheelchair had some radar device guiding it carefully down one step at a time. So much had gone wrong that evening that Mrs. Vogel barely glanced in our direction. Most of her attention was directed to the people in the audience who were limping, walking and wheeling their way out with their pockets as full of cash as when they had arrived. She took up the mike and begged them to stay. She said that all this had been a little test of Satan's.

I wheeled Mary Frances around the outside of the tent until I found Malcolm standing at the light switch out back. I leaned down and said to Mary Frances, "You're never going to get anything but blame for this job, Mary Frances, but I think you ought to get an Oscar for special effects."

Mary Frances said, "They promised me forty-two dollars and carfare."

I took the pocketbook from the back of the wheelchair and opened it. "How much is carfare?" I asked.

"Three seventy-five plus the add-on for after dark. That's four dollars and twenty-five cents plus one dollar tolls makes it five twenty-five."

I found a wallet in the pocketbook. There were hundreds

of dollars in it. Malcolm said, "That's a total of forty-seven dollars and twenty-five cents." And I removed exactly that amount and handed it to Mary Frances. Malcolm told her to sign a receipt for tax purposes. I found an old spiral notebook in the purse and wrote out a receipt that we had Mary Frances sign.

"That lady ought to be grateful to have my autograph," she said.

"Maybe so," I said, "but for now, I don't think she will want too many reminders of your act."

Mary Frances said, "I would like to shake your hands, but I don't think I ought to take the time to look for them."

I told her to just blow us a kiss goodbye, and she did.

I opened the pocketbook again, took the package of Herbert Tareyton cigarettes from it, tossed it back onto the seat of the wheelchair and said, "Papillon!"

Tallulah says, "*Kissing is the handshake of show business.*"

four

WE WERE BACK at Rahab Station. Tallulah was lying across her pillow-laden sofa, smoking and absent-mindedly stroking a large Dalmatian that was lying on a mound of pillows that had been tossed on the floor. Around its neck, exactly where Malcolm had detected the worn fur, the dog was wearing a collar studded with sparkling stones. The dog got up and greeted us, wagging its tail like any ordinary pet.

"So he was just a decoy," Malcolm said.

Tallulah looked up lazily. "His name is Spot."

I said, "I thought you would give a dog a more creative name than that."

"It suits him," Tallulah said. The dog finished sniffing us and lay down on the pillows again, and Tallulah resumed stroking its back. "Did you bring me my cigarettes?"

I handed them to her. She examined the pack, counting. "Fourteen. They should get me through dinner time." With long, red-tipped fingers she pulled a cigarette out of the pack and put it into her black cigarette holder. "Malcolm," she said, "a gentleman always offers a lady a light."

"I don't think you should smoke."

It was funny that Malcolm who never worried about his health did not like the idea of someone else smoking. I didn't mind it at all.

"When I want health advice, darling, I'll haunt the Mayo Clinic. Now, be a gentleman and light Tallulah's cigarette."

Malcolm lit her cigarette, and she inhaled deeply, held the smoke for a long, long time and then blew a perfect smoke ring up toward the ceiling. "Tell me what you did Topside," she said.

We told her, and she laughed. She roared. Her laugh was like a chorus of amens. Between us, we managed to relate every detail of what had happened, and Tallulah said, "I'm glad that you paid Mary Frances her forty-two dollars and carfare. Poor darling, she never made it to the big time. Bad marriages." She sat bolt upright and addressed Malcolm. "Now if you want to talk about bad habits, darling, you just have an in-depth conversation with Mary Frances. She can fill a Rolodex with bad habits. I can think of four to file under the letter S alone." She relaxed again and smiled, half to herself. "But she can act, can't she?"

Seeing how much she enjoyed our account of what happened, I asked her why she didn't come with us.

"I can't do a thing Topside, darling. I'm incorporeal. I'm just a whiff of a thing. No body. No body at all."

44

"Then what are we seeing?" I turned to Malcolm. "You see her, don't you, Malcolm? You see a person. A body."

Malcolm nodded.

Tallulah said. "Don't worry, Jeanmarie. Of course, you see me. That first box you passed through, the Epigene, enables you to see the unseen, and the Orgone makes you invisible." She saw that I still looked uneasy. "Relax, darling. That first lavendor box—beautiful, wasn't it?" We nodded. "That's the Epigene. It enables you to see the incorporeal— that's me, darling—and the Orgone makes you invisible. Simple."

I asked her if she thought Carl E. Vogel would give up his phony ministry.

"For a while. Before he became a faith healer, he sold medical school diplomas, and before that, he sold licorice-flavored sugar water as arthritis medicine. He does seem to enjoy bilking the sick and disabled. I just hope that Sisters Booth and Love find work elsewhere. Did you like their singing?" We said that we did. "I'm glad, darlings. They're real country." She crossed one blue satin leg over the other and said. "I imagine that it's getting late. I think you better return Topside." She instructed us to walk downstage and to stand perfectly still under the hood that would suck us back up through the Epigene. As we started to walk away, she called out to us, "Remember to take your shovels, darlings. Tallulah cannot think what she would do with them except they might make cute earrings for King Kong." She waved to us as we waited to be transported back through the Epigene and said that she would have Spot play dead again when she was ready for us to have our second trial.

45

☙ ☙ ☙

WE CHECKED Jericho Tel after school every day. On Saturday, when Mother and I did grocery shopping and laundry, I saw Malcolm and his father at the laundromat. We exchanged a few words and learned that neither one of us would have a chance to visit Jericho Tel that day. I watched Mr. Soo folding laundry. Even their underjerseys were folded with knifelike edges, and their wash was white enough for a TV commercial. I would be embarrassed to have my laundry look that good; people would think that mother and I had nothing better to do with our time.

As Mother and I left the laundromat, I saw a line at the movie. *The Exorcist* was playing; it was about a young girl who is possessed by the devil and begins to vomit green and pee on the carpet in front of her mother's guests. Not any ordinary carpet but an Oriental rug. There had been stories in the newspaper about people passing out right in the theater because some scenes in the movie were so gross. Of course, everyone at school was talking about having seen *The Exorcist*, going to see it or wanting to. No one under seventeen was allowed in without being accompanied by an adult. I saw Lynette Hrivnak, who was queen of the sixth grade clones, and two members of her court standing in line to get in; they had somebody's big brother with them. It must have been a big brother because one of the clones looked like him, and the others were admiring his pimples.

Mother asked me if I would like to go with her to see the movie, but I said that I didn't want to stand in line. There was no point in telling her that I had heard enough about the movie to know that I would vomit. It might not be green, but it would be disgusting.

On Sunday, Mother and I had an early dinner together before she left. I had finished washing up the dishes and was feeling less lonely than I usually did when Mother had to work on Sunday. I was even slightly anxious for her to go because I had Jericho Tel to look forward to. I wandered over there, half hoping that Spot would be there, and a little worried that he would be, for I was not sure that Malcolm would be able to get away, and I did not think I was ready to venture into Rahab Station without him.

When I saw Spot lying there smack in the middle of Jericho Tel, all my doubts about whether or not I wanted to return vanished. My heart started pounding, and I started running out of the Tel to get my shovel. I immediately ran back and said to Spot, "I'll be right back. Stay, Spot. Stay. Jeanmarie's going to get her shovel. Jeanmarie will be right back." I was one past excited; I was thrilled. I hoped Malcolm could come, but there was no way that I would not go even if he couldn't. I raced to Malcolm's house, swallowed hard and told my heart to calm down before I walked up the two steps to knock on his door. Mr. Soo answered.

"Is Malcolm home?" I asked.

"Yes. He is in shower bath. You like to come in and wait?"

"No, thank you. But would you please tell him that I have spotted our next assignment?"

"Okay. I tell him."

"Please tell him now and please use those very words: I have *spotted* our next assignment."

47

"For what class, miss?"

I thought. "Tell him . . . tell him . . . for Jericho's. Will you tell him that?"

Mr. Soo said that he would, and I ran home to get my shovel, worried that if I did not move quickly, Spot would not still be there when I returned. I had no way of knowing how long he had been waiting for me to find him. There is nothing more frustrating than having to do two things at once except having to hurry doing them. I hated rushing more than anything. I often wished that I lived in a time when it took so long to do things—like washing clothes or getting from one place to another—that the doing of them in itself was an accomplishment. Of course, if that were so, then there wouldn't be airports and my mother wouldn't have a job, and our family wash would look ghastly.

Maybe I had slowed down enough or maybe Malcolm had hurried up enough, but he was there, shovel in hand, by the door of his trailer when I got there.

Together we raced to Jericho Tel.

Spot was waiting, no longer lying down, playing dead, but sitting up. He started wagging his tail as soon as we reached the opening. As soon as we were within the opening, we felt ourselves being swept toward center. We wanted to enter Rahab Station together, so we poked our shovels into the ground at the count of three. They hardly made contact with the earth when we felt ourselves being sucked down until we landed on top of the Epigene. Spot followed, and as soon as his four paws hit the lavender lid, the box opened, and we tumbled down, down, down through the Epigene until we landed on our feet, facing Tallulah in her blue satin pajamas, lying in her nest of pastel satin pillows, holding Spot's collar.

She seemed glad to see us.

"I'm just delighted, darlings, that you were available this evening. My dear, dear friend, Horace Livermore, is dining with his fiancée, Isobel Wooton, at The Left Bank, an absolutely fabulous restaurant in New York. The food is divine." She buckled Spot's collar around his neck and patted his rump. "I hope you'll bring back a doggie bag for Spot. He's dying—forgive the expression—for some red meat, poor creature."

Malcolm said, "Well, aren't you going to tell us our assignment?"

"Don't be pushy, darling."

"Last time, you at least told us who it was. Aren't you even going to tell us that much."

"No, darling. This test is a little bit harder, you see."

"I'd say it's a lot harder."

"Yes, that's the nature of most tests. Not screen tests, however. The acting got easier and easier. The only problem was the camera got harsher and harsher. I have never thought it fair that by the time I could play any age at all—having been through them all—the only thing the camera picked up was an old lady. I'll never forgive the camera for that. The camera does lie, darlings. It never sees the girl within the woman, and that girl is always there. Remember that whenever you see an old lady. There's still part of her that is just twelve years old." She tore the wrapping off a fresh pack of cigarettes.

"I see that you have a large supply of cigarettes," I said.

"Yes, darling, they're bootleg. No state stamps. The truck got stopped coming from North Carolina, and the highway patrol confiscated them. They used to burn them until everyone read the Surgeon General's report. Now they bury them. Spot is such a good dog at sniffing out booty. God bless him, and God bless the highway patrol for doing their job so well. I'm afraid I must ask you to bring me matches from The Left Bank. It's not that I'm asking for souvenirs, you see; that is too, too tacky for words. And Tallulah does so hate to be tacky, but she needs the matches, darlings. She really does. Do you think you could lift a dozen books of matches for old Tallulah?"

"Is that all?" Malcolm asked. "Is that all the instructions we're going to get?"

Tallulah looked at him, surprised. "I thought I made it all perfectly clear. Part of the test is finding the problem."

"You don't make much perfectly clear, Tallulah."

"*Au contraire, mon cheri*, I think I do."

"We better go now," I said.

"Do you remember what the pretty word is that will bring you back to Rahab Station?" We nodded. "*Papillon!* it is, my dears. Ta-taaaah!" she called. "Remember upstage left and through the Orgone."

❦ ❦ ❦

THE TABLES were covered with soft apricot-colored cloths, and in the center of each table was a vase of fresh flowers: iris, pink carnations and a single yellow rose. Along the side wall and the back there were booths that faced into the room, not deep ones that cut across the room like the ones at a Mc-

Donald's. Some could seat only two, and none could seat more than six. I found myself studying the room, taking my time, not feeling at all rushed about finding out what we were supposed to do, not even feeling worried about knowing which two of the fifty or sixty people in the restaurant were Horace Livermore and Isobel Wooton. I felt again that sensation of freedom, that sensation that I was watching this person, Jeanmarie Troxell, who was simply wonderful and would do everything right.

At a stand in the front of the restaurant stood a man in a tuxedo. A customer approached and said, "Good evening, Dvorak." Dvorak said, "Good evening, Mr. Williams." He looked briefly in the large appointment book that was open on top of the stand and said, "A party of four this evening?" The man nodded. Dvorak called another man over and said, "Mr. Williams to table seven, please." Three other people who had been taking off their coats and giving them to the woman in the coatroom joined Mr. Williams, and away they went following the second man.

Next to the open book stood a large clear glass bowl filled with matches that said The Left Bank in gold print on navy blue. Malcolm reached in and took out a handful, and Dvorak, who was making notes in his appointment book, looked up and saw the matches leaving the bowl, looked down and then quickly up again. (Tallulah would tell us later that what Dvorak did was called "a double take.") Malcolm put the matches into his pocket, but to all the world, and most especially to Dvorak, they looked as if they were floating three feet above the ground. I realized that Dvorak was seeing the part of Malcolm that had not been exposed to the Orgone. We could not accomplish our mission if he didn't get rid of those matches; they were like his waving a flag wherever he went. So I took the matches out of his pocket and put them back in the bowl. Dvorak stared, shook his head, stared some more, put his pen down and went to the bar.

As soon as Dvorak left his station, I took his place. I studied the Reservations Book and saw *Williams - 4* and beside that the number 7 was circled. From what I had heard, I understood what it meant: Mr. Williams had reserved a table for four and had been assigned to table seven. Looking further up on the page, I spotted, *Livermore - 2* with the number 12 circled. Livermore, party of two, table twelve. I felt very pleased with myself until I turned to find table twelve and realized that the table numbers were known to the waiters and the captain, but they weren't written anywhere for me to see. But I didn't despair. If Mr. Williams had been seated at table seven, table twelve would be only five away from that. I didn't know in which direction, but the old confidence that I had felt from the minute I had become invisible was with me again, and I beckoned to Malcolm to follow me.

We walked over to table seven, and I looked around. Five tables away in one direction was a party of six. It was easy to eliminate them. In all other directions the tables were occupied by parties of two, and at one of those there was a gray-haired gentleman who wore a scarf instead of a necktie, with a companion, a slightly overweight woman who was studying him adoringly. She wore a killer diamond on the plump third finger of her left hand and a pale green dress with a pattern of yellow rings in the fabric—the color and pattern of a luna moth.

Malcolm and I exchanged a look and a nod, letting each other know that we had located Horace Livermore and his fiancée, Isobel Wooton. We arrived at their table in time to hear the man say, "Are you sure you can't come to California? The time away will do you good, my dear."

"I can't, Horace. If I leave Jason at all, Victor will haul me into court and try to get custody."

"But surely, darling, a short vacation does not constitute child neglect."

"You know that the judge will not look kindly on my keeping company with another man."

The waiter cleared their plates and asked if they would like coffee. Both said yes, and Isobel said that she was going to powder her nose before the coffee came. She picked up her pocketbook and, with her free hand, reached across the table and squeezed Horace's hand before heading in the direction of the ladies' room. I followed.

Malcolm followed the waiter, hoping to get the scraps from their plates for Spot.

I wondered if in my invisible state I could walk through closed doors. I didn't want to injure myself finding out, so I followed Isobel very closely and managed to slip through the door just behind her. The ladies' room consisted of two parts. A front room that had a sofa and a wall mirror and a row of seats in front of a vanity table—there was free Kleenex everywhere—and a separate room that had toilet booths; there were only two. The room with the toilets also had two beautiful sinks of a kind of marble that looked like coffee ripple ice cream. There was a glass shelf and a mirror above each of the sinks. Sitting on a stool in a corner between the two rooms was a woman wearing a plain black dress with white

53

collar and cuffs and a small white apron. On the counter near the doorway was a dish that had two one dollar bills in it. I had never been to a restaurant where they had a baby-sitter in the bathroom.

Isobel was the only person using the facilities. She nodded to the baby-sitter as she went into one of the booths, but she didn't stay long or even flush before she came out and started washing her hands at one of the marble sinks. The woman handed her a cloth towel, and Isobel took it, thanked her and then reached into her pocketbook and took out a dollar and laid it on the dish. I heard the sound of metal hitting china and thought that Isobel must have given her some change as well. The woman said thank you and nodded.

I looked at the bill and saw that it was not one dollar but ten. The woman quickly put the bill and the coin in her apron pocket, and I decided that I better stay and see what the ladies' room attendant was going to do, so I sat down on the sofa in the first of the two rooms where I could watch everyone who came in as well as the baby-sitter herself.

Two customers came in shortly after Isobel finished. They left fifty cents apiece. The woman removed those coins from the plate and walked out, heading toward the kitchen. I followed. She took a cup of coffee and found a place in the far corner of the kitchen where she sat down and drank her coffee out of the way of the pandemonium. The whole procedure puzzled me.

I found Malcolm near the grill, trying to stab a steak. I pulled him away and walked with him to the busiest, meanest part of the kitchen, to where the waiters brought in and picked up their orders. In addition to the arguments between the waiters and the cooks, there was an enormous fan blowing, so if I kept my voice low, no one would notice that there were voices in the room that didn't belong to anybody. Any *body*.

I told Malcolm what I had seen. We thought it best to return to the restaurant because we both knew that the curtain was about to go up on the next act there.

As we passed the corridor that led to the ladies' room, we saw Isobel rushing out, back toward the restaurant. She reached the table and began to cry. Horace patted her hand, and said, "Now, now, my dear, I'm certain that we'll find it." He motioned for the waiter to come over.

"My fiancée used the washroom just now, and as is her habit, she took off her diamond ring before washing her hands. She put it down on the ledge over the sink, and I'm afraid she didn't remember to put it back on. She has just returned to the ladies' room only to find that both the ring and the attendant are gone. Surely, sir . . ."

The waiter brought the captain, the captain brought Dvorak, and each time Horace told the story, Isobel cried harder and harder.

I knew that I could solve the problem. The clunk that I had thought was a quarter had been Isobel's ring. I decided to do nothing. I wanted to see how this would finish up. Our assignment had been Horace Livermore, the playwright who had not had a hit in years and years, and his fiancée, Isobel. Our assignment had been the two of them, and I knew that it had something to do with the interaction between them.

Dvorak marched back to the ladies' room and knocked

55

on the door. He had not gotten his fist back up to knock a second time when the door opened and the attendant came out, wide-eyed, holding up Isobel's ring. "Mr. Dvorak," she said, "Mr. Dvorak, sir, I just came back from having a cup of coffee, and I was wiping around them lavatories over there, and lookit at what I found there. I don't know which of them ladies could of dropped it. Do you suppose . . ."

Dvorak grabbed it from her hand, and walking as fast as he could without calling it running, he returned triumphant to the main room. "It was an unfortunate chain of circumstances," he explained. "The ring must have fallen between the lavatories, and the attendant chose that moment to take a coffee break."

Isobel was falling all over herself with crying and putting the ring back on and hugging Horace and Dvorak. Dvorak got her coat from the checkroom, and they left. "Can we call you a cab?" he asked.

"Thank you," Horace said, "but I think a little walk in the night air might do us some good."

Malcolm and I were standing back by the reservations stand. Malcolm grabbed a bunch of matches from the glass jar and put them in his pocket, and just as Dvorak was calling his last "Goodnight," I said, "Papillon!" and we were whooshed away into the Orgone.

☙ ☙ ☙

MALCOLM stepped into Rahab Station first. He walked straight over to Tallulah and emptied his pocket into her lap. Tallulah thanked him. Turning to the dog, he said,

56

"Sorry, Spot, but I couldn't get any leftovers for you."

I was excited by what we had seen Topside. "When do you think they will realize that Horace and Isobel left without paying?" I asked.

"Just about now, darling," Tallulah said, pleased.

"Why didn't anyone ask why Isobel didn't find the ring when she returned to the ladies' room just before she broke down in tears."

Tallulah shrugged. "Isobel is a wonderful actress, and Horace always did write the best dialogue around."

Malcolm asked, "Will they mail him the bill once they realize that no one paid?"

"I doubt it, darling. They would have to mention why it was overlooked, and mentioning it would be embarrassing."

"How about that? The Left Bank food at McDonald's prices."

I said, "Once I saw what was going on, there was no way in the world I would have told on them. I just knew that even though they were wrong, it would have been more wrong to tell on them. Someday, when I'm Topside and visible, I would like to meet Horace and Isobel and her son Jason."

"Isobel Wooton has no son named Jason. I told you Horace Livermore writes the most convincing dialogue in the world. Now, Malcolm, be a gentleman and pick up those matches and light up one of Tallulah's bootleggings for her."

Malcolm muttered something about cigarettes being coffin nails, and Tallulah said, "They don't nail coffins these days, darling. I think they sealed mine with silly putty."

❧ ❧ ❧

As we walked back toward home, I started to worry. When I was invisible, I saw everything so clearly, yet I had believed that Isobel had a son named Jason. How stupid of me not to have known.

I did not have a chance to worry out loud, for at that moment Malcolm realized that he did not have his right hand.

"The matches!" he said. "I put the matches in my pocket and kept my hand in my pocket when we went through the Orgone. And now my hand is gone."

"Pat my head, Malcolm," I commanded.

Malcolm did.

"Shake my hand, Malcolm."

Malcolm did.

"The hand's there. I can feel it. It just remained invisible."

"What am I supposed to do?"

"Come back to my house. My mother is not home. We'll think of something."

Tallulah says, *"The difference between going to school and getting an education is the difference between picking an apple and eating it."*

five

ONCE HE WAS certain that his hand was available even though it was invisible, Malcolm began to enjoy the possibilities. "I can pick my nose in class."

"You still have to get rid of the boogers."

"I can shoot Mrs. Hollings a bird, and she won't even know."

"Then what's the point of shooting her one?"

"I can rob a bank and not leave fingerprints."

"You're not old enough to drive. They'll catch you leaving the scene of the crime on foot."

"What would you do if you had one invisible hand?"

"Try to think of some way to keep everyone from finding out about it. We can't let anyone else find out about Jericho Tel. Not yet. Maybe not ever."

Malcolm held up his arm. "I don't know what to do, Jeanmarie. If I skip school, my father will find out. If I go to school, everyone else will."

It came to me in a flash. "Wear a glove. Wear a glove. That's it, Malcolm. You know your hand is there. You shook hands with me." I ran back to my room and came out with a mitten and told him to put it on.

When he did, the mitten did not look empty. It moved when he did. "I can't write with a mitten," he said.

"You could with a glove. Don't you have a glove?"

"Of course I have a glove. But what will I tell my father?" Malcolm thought a minute. "I can go straight to bed when I go home, and I can probably keep him from seeing my hand in the morning because he goes to work before I go to school. If we get a call from Jericho Tel tomorrow, I can keep my father from finding out, but what will I do about school?"

"Skip it," I said.

"I can't do that," Malcolm said.

"Why not?"

"I'm an immigrant."

"So what?"

"Immigrants are always overachievers."

I said, "I'll think of something. I'll call you. Just remember, when I call, pick up the receiver with your left hand."

After Malcolm waved goodbye with his handless right arm, I took *Dr. Maceo E. Patterson's Home Encyclopedia of Medicine* down from the shelf and did some serious research. I had never before spoken to Malcolm on the phone. I looked his number up in the phone book; there was only one Soo in the entire directory. Tyrone Soo. That must be his father, I thought, although I had expected his father to have an untranslated immigrant name like Sung or Choong. I dialed the number and hoped that Malcolm would answer. I preferred not having to explain to Mr. Tyrone Soo who I was and who I wanted to speak to and why.

The phone rang only once, and Malcolm answered. I regarded that as a good sign. "Listen," I said, holding the phone right up against my mouth and speaking very softly into it, "You can have impetigo, eczema or poison ivy. Impetigo is contagious—highly contagious—and has pustules that burst and form a yellow crust. Eczema is not contagious and has redness, itching and breaks in the skin that seep and form a crust. I don't know if that crust is yellow. Poison ivy is a rash that forms red streaks of pimples that itch. It is not contagious."

"I think I'll take impetigo."

"That was going to be my recommendation. I think that a contagious disease is the best kind. Then, if Mrs. Hollings threatens to take your glove, you can tell her that she's endangering the health of innocent children."

"Would you spell it for me?"

I did, checking the picture of it in Dr. Maceo E. Patterson's encyclopedia. "It's gross, Malcolm. Really gross."

❦ ❦ ❦

THE FOLLOWING morning I waited just inside my door until I saw Malcolm on his way to the bus stop. He waved to me with his right hand; he was wearing one white cotton gardener's glove.

"What happened to your hand, Malcolm?" I asked.

"Impetigo. A grossly contagious disease."

"Do you have any idea how long it lasts?"

"It could last as long as a week, or it could by some miracle be cured in a day."

ALTHOUGH Malcolm and I were in the same grade, we were not in the same homeroom. Ever since the day of the blue jay, I had gotten into the habit of looking for him every time we changed classes. I expected to find him leaving the library as I was entering and entering the cafetorium as I was leaving. Even though we never spoke, I looked forward to seeing him even for just a glance during the course of the day. When he did not show up at library or lunch, I got worried.

There was no one in his homeroom that I would ask.

All the sixth grades shared the same gym period, and when Malcolm did not show up for that either, I asked to be excused to go to the girls' room and went instead to the office.

I asked the school secretary if she could please tell me what had happened to Malcolm Soo. The secretary asked me the nature of my interest. I told her that I had found his house key and wanted to return it to him.

"You ought not to touch that key," the secretary said.

I took my own key from around my neck and dangled it in front of the woman. She leaned away from it. "You better be careful. Malcolm Soo has a dread disease, and it is my duty to advise you to sterilize anything that has so much as touched that boy's body."

I asked where he was, and the secretary told me that he was in the infirmary and had been all day. "He would have been sent home if there had been someone at home to receive him. I can tell you that he will not be allowed back in this building without a signed certificate from a doctor. I can't imagine a father letting a child come to school with something as dreadful as impelliago disease."

"Im-pet-EYE-go," I corrected.

"I tell you, these foreigners have no sense of responsibility. They come into this country and take, take, take. They take jobs and welfare and what do they give us in return? Impelliago! It's a disgrace."

I felt that little knot between my eyes snap, and I said, "It's a shame that Malcolm Soo never told you how he got the disease."

"I'm sure he got it from the filthy conditions they live in."

"Not quite," I said. "Every weekend he and his father Tyrone volunteer to be infected with a different disease so that researchers can test different medicines to see what could cure it."

"Well, that is nice of them saving all those poor dogs and unfortunate mice from having to get infected." She stopped, squinted at me and asked, "Or do they get paid for doing it? I have no use for people who give blood for money."

"No, they don't get paid. He and Tyrone are part of the Infect an Immigrant Program. When the whole study is finished, they are getting a trip to Washington, D.C., where they're going to get the Dr. Maceo E. Patterson Award for their contribution to scientific medicine. Usually, the disease disappears before he has to return to school, but this weekend it didn't. Malcolm has suffered the pains of Hell on weekends."

"Don't you say 'Hell' to me, young lady."

63

"Can I have a pass to go to the infirmary?"

"I'd advise against it, if you want my opinion."

"I don't know how he'll get the key to his house if I don't give it to him." I dangled the key right up close to her face.

She leaned far back from it and wrote out the pass. She stood back as I lifted the barrier to enter the inner office and then beyond that into the room just to the side of the principal's office that they called the infirmary.

Malcolm was lying on the cot, holding a book in the space over his face, reading.

I collapsed onto the cot. "I can't believe what I just did," I said. I told him what I had told the secretary. "I wasn't scared at all. It was as if the invisible part of me made it up. I wasn't scared for a single minute."

As he listened, Malcolm laid his opened book across his chest and put his hands behind his head. "The good news is that I picked impetigo, and it's so rotten that they didn't even want to peek inside my glove. The bad news is that I picked impetigo, and it's so rotten that they want me to have a doctor's certificate before I come back. How am I supposed to get that?"

"If we don't get a call to Jericho Tel, and you have to miss school tomorrow, I'll bring you your assignments."

"You're not listening to me, Jeanmarie. How am I supposed to get a doctor's certificate?"

"Let's just hope we get a call back to Jericho Tel."

Malcolm sat up. Slowly, slowly, one finger at a time, he pulled the glove from his right hand. Then making a menacing face, and lifting his arms in batwing fashion, he grabbed my throat with his invisible hand. "You see, my dear, there are many advantages to being slight of hand."

Tallulah says, "*A star should demand three things in her contract: her name above the title, a limousine to take her to and from the theater and fresh Belgian chocolates in her dressing room. If she doesn't want the chocolates, then she should demand free hospitalization, for it's certain that she's crazy.*"

six

As SOON as we got off the bus, we dumped our books, picked up our shovels and headed for Jericho Tel. We peered anxiously through the trees, and to our great joy and relief saw Spot, wagging his tail just inside the opening to Jericho Tel.

One, two, three, and we were through the Epigene and standing in Rahab Station. Tallulah looked up lazily when we arrived.

The first thing I said was, "Malcolm needs a hand."

"Of course, darling!" Tallulah said. She clamped her cigarette holder between her teeth and started clapping. "Tallulah knows that getting a hand is not always easy."

"Not that! Not *a* hand. *His* hand. He left it in his pocket in the Orgone, and it remained invisible Topside."

"Oh, darling," Tallulah said. "That kind of hand is so

much easier for Tallulah to get for you. Don't worry about it, darling. Show it to Tallulah." Malcolm extended his gloved hand. "Take that tacky glove off, darling. What kind of glove is that?" Malcolm told her that it was a gardener's glove. "A gardener's glove?" she asked.

"It keeps dirt from getting under your fingernails when you work in the garden." Malcolm explained.

"I'm sure that if God had meant people to wear gloves while working in a garden, He would have made Adam and Eve a pair out of fig leaves."

"People who garden as a hobby and have to keep their fingernails clean for other things wear gardener's gloves when they garden."

"You don't say? I had a house with a garden once. Everyone kept telling me, 'Tallulah, with a dog, you should have a garden. It's not fair to keep a dog cooped up in a city apartment all the time.' So my then Spot—I've always had a Dalmatian, and I've always called him Spot; it gives one a sense of continuity—and I moved to a place in Connecticut. I've been told the garden was beautiful. Tallulah can tell you if a diamond necklace is beautiful, and she has simply fabulous taste in clothing, but gardens, darling, are just not in Tallulah's line.

"Fiona, who was my housekeeper and cook, was delighted, and so was Widdup, her husband, who was my chauffeur and butler. Widdup loved to garden; the English have a passion for it. One day Widdup told me that he would like to plant a vegetable garden so that Fiona could have things fresh from the garden to cook. I told him that it was perfectly all right with me as long as I didn't have to hire migrant labor; I had heard all these perfectly awful stories about the terrible houses that migrant labor lives in, and I didn't want to have to put up any dilapidated houses for them. It would make the place look just too tacky. Widdup assured me that he would manage the whole thing all by himself, so he went out and bought all these precious little plants and dug around—it seemed to me that he was busy for days—and invited me out into the garden to look.

"It was all very cute, I must say. He had put all these tiny plants into the ground in wonderful straight rows. There were little labels sticking out of the ground at the end of each row. I read the pictures on the labels and saw that there was a row of radishes and something yellow and something green. They all seemed to start out green, come to think of it. I complimented Widdup on his beautiful garden and didn't pay any more attention until he came to me one day and told me he had to fertilize. I said, 'Go right ahead, darling,' but he said that he needed money for the fertilizer, that he wanted me to open an account at the local hardware store. I asked him what he was going to fertilize with, and when he told me manure, I told him that we wouldn't have to buy any, that we could just let my then Spot loose in the garden, and he would take care of everything. Widdup said, 'No, Madam, we need good cow manure.' Well, there I was in the city, not able to give the stuff away, and there I was in the country, having to buy somebody else's. I decided that gardening was just too complicated a pastime, so I sold the house and the garden, and we all moved back into the city."

I told Tallulah about the time when Mother and I had lived in Texas and had tried growing tomatoes outside our trailer and about the bugs that ooze green slime when you step on them; and Tallulah said, "So much of Nature is green; there must be a reason for it."

At that point Malcolm explained chlorophyll and photosynthesis. He started explaining energy cycles when Tallulah interrupted, "Now, now, Malcolm, let's not get carried away. Good explanations are like bathing suits, darling; they are meant to reveal everything by covering only what is necessary."

"Do you have a new assignment for us?" I asked.

Tallulah said, "It's time I told you your quest."

"Not yet," Malcolm said.

"Why not yet?" Tallulah asked.

"Because we have had only two trials. There's always three."

"Who says there's always three?"

"Everyone. There's always three brothers who start out. There's always three wishes. There's always three. Even when people tell jokes, there's always a minister, a priest and a rabbi."

Tallulah said, "Don't be such a technician, darling. Why don't you just rejoice that your trials are over and you are about to embark on your real mission."

"I've enjoyed the trials."

"Of course you did, darling, but Tallulah is convinced that you already know what you need to." She held up her hands and pulled her little finger down with the forefinger of her other hand. "One, you've distinguished the real from the phony." She gazed off into space. "Now let me see, what comes next." She pulled down her next finger. "Oh, yes. Two. You've also decided that doing nothing is sometimes

68

doing something. One. Two. You're ready for your mission."

It was then that I reminded Tallulah that I had believed Horace and Isobel, that I had really thought that she had a son named Jason, and, furthermore, I had not even realized that her diamond was not real, and how all that made me wonder if I really could distinguish the real from the phony. Tallulah told me to shush. "Darling, darling," she said, "if you could distinguish the real from the phony and also distinguish the real from the magic, I would not think you were at all ready. Tallulah wants you to believe that magic is real. You've proven yourselves to my entire satisfaction, and Tallulah is anxious for you to find The Regina Stone. Really she is."

Malcolm looked unhappy, but if Tallulah noticed, she paid no attention. "Now Tallulah will tell you your quest," she said.

❧ ❧ ❧

THE FOLLOWING is my account of Tallulah's account of our mission.

Three years before she died, Tallulah had gone to an exhibition at the Metropolitan Museum of Art in New York. As she was coming down the steps, she heard a lovely voice singing "Greensleeves." The singer was a beautiful young woman quaintly dressed in a long-sleeved calico pinafore made with half a hundred hand-sewn tucks. She wore an amusing straw hat with a fresh carnation in its band and kept a small straw basket near her feet for people to drop money into. Tallulah listened until the girl finished her song

69

and then dropped a twenty dollar bill into her hat, but not before she had written *Brava!* and her name and phone number on it.

Two days later the girl called Tallulah and introduced herself. Her name was Emmagene Krebs. Tallulah suggested that they meet for lunch at the Plaza. The girl told Tallulah that she had come from Kokomo, Indiana, to make her name and find her fortune in New York. She said that she was eighteen years old and had eighteen thousand songs to sing. She showed Tallulah a big notebook where, at the end of each day, she listed the songs that she had sung that day and counted down from eighteen thousand. At the time they met, she had sixteen thousand eight hundred and twelve songs left. "Greensleeves" was one of her favorites. "Scarlet Ribbons" was another. She had six other favorites, and every day she allowed herself to sing one of those eight plus four or five other songs. She said that when she had only one hundred songs left to sing, she would sing only her eight favorites. What she wanted more than anything was to be discovered so that she could give concerts at Carnegie Hall or Lincoln Center so that more people could hear her songs before she had no more songs to sing.

Tallulah found herself very interested in the young busker. Her New York apartment was not far from the Metropolitan Museum, and she took to walking her then Spot to the museum and waiting with him while Emmagene Krebs sang. Sometimes if she and Spot arrived close to the time that Emmagene was finishing her songs for that day, they would walk back to the apartment together, where Widdup would serve them a cup of tea. Tallulah always asked Emmagene if she wanted Fiona to put honey in her tea to save her voice. Emmagene always said no, that she knew she had eighteen thousand songs to sing, and she was counting down, and nothing, nothing at all, could make her have eighteen thousand and one, but what she wanted was a bigger audience so that more people could hear her songs.

After a while Emmagene told Tallulah that she had a good friend who was a ventriloquist named Nicolai Ion Simonescu. She shyly told Tallulah that Nicolai was in love with her. He was also a street performer; his dummy's name was Anna Karenina. Tallulah said that she would love to meet Nicolai and his Anna. Emmagene said that she would bring him by some Monday, the day when most of street performers did not work.

The following Monday Emmagene did bring Nicolai, and Nicolai brought his dummy, Anna Karenina. Nicolai performed some of his routine for Tallulah, and Tallulah loved it, and she liked Anna Karenina very much, too, so they started joining Emmagene when she visited Tallulah at her apartment. Nicolai said that he would like to get on television. He worried that he would grow old and arthritic and unable to pull Anna Karenina's strings before he was discovered.

Soon Nicolai brought Patrick Henry Mermelstein to their Monday afternoon tea parties. Patrick Henry, whom most people called P.H., booked himself as Mermelstein the Magician. Mermelstein the Magician's specialty was sleight-of-hand. It was supposed to be that: Mermelstein might be a magician, but Patrick Henry was a klutz. He dropped things. Coins that were meant to appear from behind someone's ear would fall to the floor, and a long string of scarves that was to be pulled out of a hat would become tangled. P.H. managed to keep up a lighthearted patter as Mermelstein failed at one magical trick after another. He carried a tape player with him and played classical music as he went through his routine. He liked Mozart most of all.

One day Tallulah was walking her then Spot in Shubert Alley when she stopped to see Mermelstein the Magician doing card tricks. He was in the middle of asking someone in his audience to pick a card when he stopped, said, "Wait a minute now. Here comes the sound of real magic." At that point he cocked his ear toward the tape recorder until the musical passage was over and then picked up his patter without missing a beat, but he did drop the deck of cards he was shuffling. Many people helped to pick them up, and Tallulah saw that even though most of his audience left without waiting for Mermelstein to finish his trick, a few had dropped coins and bills into his top hat. P.H. wanted to take his act to Las Vegas, where he hoped to become a headliner at some of the big casinos there. The money was terrific, and thousands of people would see him every night.

Sometimes other buskers would show up at the Monday afternoon teas. Once P.H. brought The Tumbleweeds, three young men who could juggle anything you gave them including a kitchen chair; and once Nicolai brought Victor and Viv, two mimes who worked so closely together that even when they were sitting around Tallulah's living room having tea, they crossed their legs at the same time. But the three who came every Monday, week in and week out, were Emmagene Krebs, Nicolai Ion Simonescu and Patrick Henry Mermelstein. And Anna Karenina if you wanted to count her.

All of the street performers that Tallulah came to know shifted around from one part of the city to another, keeping track of each other and often guarding their corner of the park or what they considered their spot on the sidewalk. The classical musicians preferred uptown locations: the steps of the museum, the street in front of St. Patrick's Cathedral or the area around the new Lincoln Center. The more acrobatic performers liked to be downtown at Washington Square. In between were people like Nicolai and Patrick Henry who could collect an audience almost anywhere, but who most preferred to be in Shubert Alley in the theater district.

Besides having some locations that were better than others, the seasoned performers knew that there were some times that were more profitable than others. These were when movies and plays were starting or letting out. In Washington Square, the best times were on bright Saturday and Sunday afternoons when tourists flooded the streets to see the life of Greenwich Village. There was an unwritten code among the regulars that they take turns at the best times and places, though those who had been performing on the streets for years had the right to claim the best times and the best places for themselves. They were sometimes as unfriendly to new street acts as the rich and famous entertainers were to them. A few of the established street performers had their own groupies.

Tallulah and her then Spot made the rounds of the city, greeting the buskers she knew personally. She often stood still to watch a performance from beginning to end, after which she would drop something substantial into the hat and go on her way. And every Monday she looked forward to the visit of Emmagene, Nicolai, Mermelstein the Magician and Anna Karenina, if you wanted to count her. They had all become Tallulah's darlings.

Winter is a bad time for street performers. When the weather is very bad, they cannot work out of doors, for no one wants to stand around watching or listening when it is freezing. Emmagene, Nicolai and P.H. sometimes had weeks at a time when they could not work, and they became restless. Emmagene complained that she now had only fifteen thousand nine hundred and six songs left to sing, and there was no one hearing her songs.

Nicolai hired himself out entertaining children at birthday parties. He said that he had to build another dummy. As much as he loved Anna Karenina, he could see that her appeal to children was very limited; that only very bright children found her funny. His new dummy would be a frog, a pig or a big bird because he thought one of them might be more popular. P.H. got a job helping his uncle with the Christmas rush at his music store in Forest Hills, Queens. The store was called The Magic Flute after one of Mozart's operas. Everyone in P.H.'s family loved Mozart, music and magic, but not necessarily in that order. Emmagene got a part-time job as a waitress at Chock Full o'Nuts where she could save her voice for what was left of her eighteen thousand songs.

Between Thanksgiving and Christmas Tallulah seldom saw Nicolai or Patrick Henry. Since Emmagene kept more regular hours, she managed to drop by Tallulah's apartment at least once a week. Tallulah was happy for Emmagene's company, but she missed the others. It was the *us* of them that she missed. There was some magic when the four of them were together that was weakened when there was one less—or even when there was one more. Nicolai and P.H. loved performing so much that there were times during the Christmas season, when the stores were open late and the streets were full of shoppers at all hours, that they would rush out on the street after finishing their other jobs so that they could squeeze in a performance or two. On those days, Emmagene and Tallulah would go down to the streets to listen to their friends. Afterwards, they had an open invitation to tea at Tallulah's.

She invited the three of them—four, if you counted Anna Karenina—to a party at her apartment on Twelfth-Night, January 6, because she knew that all their holiday labors would be over by then. They were to dress as one of the Magi. Except Anna Karenina who was already dressed appropriately, since she always wore a tiara.

The Twelfth-Night party became a tradition, and every year Fiona made stuffed goose and plum pudding and all the old-fashioned holiday foods. Widdup polished the silver until it was so bright it seemed noisy, and Tallulah ordered a centerpiece of pine cones and green velvet ribbons. She kept the lights low and burned votive candles in a row on the mantle over the fireplace and elsewhere throughout the apartment. She had always loved to entertain, and her Twelfth-Night party for the buskers became her favorite. Every year she took her most elegant dress out of storage; it

75

was a deep ruby velvet with balloon sleeves and a long, full skirt. She had worn it on stage for her famous role of Regina, the same role that had impressed a fan so much that he had given her The Regina Stone necklace. She loved having an occasion to wear them together, for although she never took off The Regina Stone, she seldom had an opportunity to wear it with the ruby velvet gown.

In all the years since she had owned the necklace, Tallulah had never been tempted to sell it, even though keeping it was a bother and an expense. It was so valuable that insurance on the stone cost more than her groceries—but not more than her cigarettes. But Tallulah had never sold it and never would. Because The Regina Stone was a symbol to her of her success as an actress. "Not a reminder, darling. I must make that clear. I have memories as reminders. The Regina Stone was a symbol. The difference is this: Only I can see the memories; everyone could see The Regina Stone. One could hardly not see it, darlings. It was enormous. Large enough for some people to have called it vulgar. No diamond is ever vulgar. Tallulah says it is always better to have a diamond that is large and perfect than one that is small and flawed. The Regina Stone was famous as my good luck piece. Some called it Tallulah's Talisman."

After their feast, the group went into the living room and seated themselves comfortably. Widdup served coffee, and mulled cider that they stirred with a cinnamon stick. Tallulah assigned everyone a part, and they read *Twelfth Night* by William Shakespeare. The whole evening had come to be one of celebration and reunion for the buskers and Tallulah.

The evening of their last Twelfth-Night, they had finished dinner and had just been served coffee in the living room when Tallulah had her attack. She remembered feeling The Regina Stone as she clutched her throat just before passing out. There followed a brief period when everything was dark, a time when her spirit had not entirely left her body and she could not see. Then, when she was totally incorporeal, she looked back at the body she had lately occupied, and she saw that her throat was bare.

Someone had robbed her corpse of The Regina Stone.

"Your job, darlings," Tallulah said, "is to find The Regina Stone. My spirit will have no rest until you do. If you'll come to Jericho Tel straight from school, I shall send Spot Topside when I need you. Don't bother with those grimy shovels anymore; they might dirty up my divan. Just tap three times. Actually, tapping once or twice will be enough, but Malcolm seems to find some comfort in three's, so tap three times, and I'll let you down. You'll begin tomorrow. But Malcolm, darling, before you go Topside, you better give yourself a little spin in the Orgone. Jeanmarie and I will wait for you. Remember to say '*Papillon!*' when you are ready to return."

Malcolm left, and there were a hundred things I wanted to ask Tallulah. I wanted to ask her if anyone else had tried to find The Regina Stone and what would happen to her if we found it. I wanted to ask her how many plays she had been in and how many movies she had made. I wanted to know who her favorite leading man was and how rich she had been. And most of all I wanted to tell her that I longed

77

to be an actress. But I asked her none of those things, and I did not tell her my dream of becoming an actress. What I asked her was this: how did she get such a good line on her lipstick and how did she keep it from smearing.

She told me to powder my lips first and blot twice.

Tallulah says, *"Never have a long conversation with anyone who says 'between you and I.'"*

seven

WHEN WE visited Jericho Tel after school the following afternoon, Tallulah said it was late in the day, and we had a lot to do. She sounded crisp and unfriendly, the way people who are not naturally efficient sound when they try being efficient. As anxious as I was to be invisible again, I was annoyed at her rushing us Topside. I started to say that it was hardly our fault that we had to go to school for the best part of the day, but I had no chance to say anything before we were sent stage left and through the Orgone.

WE FOUND ourselves in a room large enough to be measured in acres. It was carpeted wall to wall and divided into cubicles not by walls but by desks and file cabinets. Hundreds

79

of people—most of them women—were sitting at typewriters. At least I thought they were typewriters until Malcolm pointed out that each typewriter was connected to a machine that erupted with sheet after sheet of green-streaked paper folding back on itself in accordion-pleated folds. These were no ordinary typewriters: these were computer terminals.

Since the days of my invisibility, both computers and I have undergone important changes, both inside and out, and for both of us the changes on the outside would be the least important but the most noticeable. These computers had no screens glowing with vinegar green light. These computers wrote on paper: They belched out words—rat-tat-tat, ra-ta-ta-tat, ra-ra-ra-tat-tat—one letter at a time while reams of paper rolled through them as if pulled by hands as invisible as mine and Malcolm's. I asked Malcolm what these people were doing.

Malcolm walked over to one of the women who was typing. He looked over her shoulder for a few minutes before returning to me. "This is an Internal Revenue Service Center."

"I don't believe that," I said. "No one here would have The Regina Stone, and besides, Internal Revenue is federal, and federal is in Washington, D.C."

"How do you know that we're not in Washington, D.C.?" he asked.

I couldn't answer that question. Malcolm returned to reading over the woman's shoulder. "We're at a Long Island zip code."

"How do you know what is a Long Island zip code? Do you think in zip codes or something? Do you close your eyes and dream of the lovely river flowing alongside thirty-two-two-one-seven? And do you think that the capital of Connecticut is six-one-four-four-three?"

"The capital of Connecticut is Hartford, and its zip code is zero-six-one something. The New England states all have zip codes that begin with zero."

"Ohio?"

"Begins with four."

"What about Pennsylvania?"

"One."

"Hollywood."

"Hollywood, Florida is three-three-zero; California is nine hundred something."

"Manhattan?"

"One hundred. Listen, Jeanmarie, we are wasting time. I happen to have this talent for numbers. It is not as if I try to remember them. It is that I don't forget them. I don't seem to be able to. The point is that we're still on Long Island, and this is a data processing center."

I was irritated. "Can you tell me why we were sent here? I thought we were going to go to Manhattan and watch the street performers. I don't see any Regina Stones around here. I don't even see any rhinestones. I don't see anything around here that interests me in the least."

Malcolm said, "I do."

"What?"

"This place is full of names. Names like Patrick Henry Mermelstein and Nicolai Ion Simonescu and Emmagene Krebs."

"So what."

"If they have the names, they also have the addresses. And if they have the addresses, we can track down all the people who were there when Tallulah died."

"Don't forget Fiona and Widdup. The butler always did it."

"What is that supposed to mean?"

"That is supposed to mean that if you read mystery novels, everyone forgets about the butler's having been in the room, just the way you forgot about Widdup's having been there. In the end, it turns out that the butler did it."

"Did what?"

"Did the murder. Of course, I'm not saying that Tallulah was murdered. I just think that you better look up the maid and the butler. They could have taken The Regina Stone as easily as anyone else. Maybe easier."

"I don't know how we're going to find Fiona. We don't have her last name."

"Her last name is Widdup."

"That's the butler's name."

"If you'd ever read an English novel, you'd know that butlers are always called by their last names, and since Fiona and Widdup were husband and wife, she must be Fiona Widdup. His first name is probably Arthur or Charles, something from the British royal family."

"How do you spell Fiona?"

I told him how and then I said, "I think that it is just too bad. I am very disappointed."

"You've known for a long time that I don't have a talent for spelling."

"That's not what I'm disappointed about. I hate to rely on a *data processing center*."

82

"If I can accept the magic, you can accept the technology. Or try to."

"I want only to have some magic in my life."

"I happen to think that going from Jericho Tel to . . ." he glanced over his shoulder to read what was coming off the teletape ". . . Holtsville in the blink of an eye is magic. Right now, I happen to feel very much at home, and I am anxious to get to work. I am going to stand behind this woman and watch what she does. You be lookout and see which of these people is going to take a coffee break." I asked him why, and he told me that as soon as he learned how to break into the system, he was going to sit at someone's place and get data out of the databank.

I was impressed. I didn't know that a databank was like a regular bank, something you had to break into. He stood behind the woman closest to us and read her fingers as they raced over the keyboard, giving commands and making requests. I saw how he concentrated so fiercely that he didn't even notice when I left to walk across the room and sit at a terminal where an operator had just left. At last he looked up and beckoned to me to follow him to a far corner of the room where we could talk a little louder without being heard.

"There's a code," he said. "Before the computer will give me information, I have to enter a password. But even before that, I have to enter an identification number. I know hers," he said, pointing to the woman he had just left. "It won't work for me to try to sit at any empty seat. We'll just have to make this woman get up and move away from her place, and you'll have to keep her away while I get the computer to tell me what I need. Can you do it?"

I said I was sure I could.

The two of us stood behind our victim. With a slight nod of his chin, Malcolm let me know that I was to begin. I tickled the back of her neck first. She squinched her head, creasing it back toward her shoulders a couple of times before I started rubbing my finger back and forth under her nose. Back and forth, back and forth. Lightly, like a hair across her face. She kept wrinkling her nose and swatting the back of her neck. Malcolm started running his fingers through her hair, and I kept doing my thing, avoiding sticking my fingers up her nose. I began blowing in her ears as well. First the right ear and then the left as I continued to rub under her nose and tickle the back of her neck. Soon she was lifting both hands from the keyboard to bat them around in the air and slap the back of her neck and rub her nose. I'm sure it was a surprise to find a finger already under her nose when she tried to rub it. Malcolm and I persisted for two or three minutes before the woman finally shook her head and said, "I think I better take a break." She diddled with the keys, the teletape shut down, and she left.

Malcolm wasted no time sliding into her chair. He reversed her diddle, and in no time at all, the teletape sent the message: LOG ON. Then Malcolm typed in some combinations of numbers and letters, and the next message it sent was PLEASE ENTER PASSWORD. I was impressed that a machine said "please." Malcolm typed something in. It must have been correct, for the next thing the computer wanted was a code. He did everything the computer asked before he made his first request. He commanded the computer to give him the 1040 forms of Nicolai Ion Simonescu, and

84

the computer had started typing out the information when the young man at the next console noticed that there was a machine operating without an operator. He called out to someone who must have been the supervisor, "Ted, there's a ghost in Murph's machine; better come shut it down."

Ted came over to Murph's machine and attempted to sit in her chair. However, everytime he lowered his buttocks, Malcolm pinched him hard. He popped up as if he had been stung—which in a way, he had been. He said to the man who had called him over. "Where in the hell is Murph? How can she walk away from a malfunction like this?"

Murph was returning from the employees' lounge when she saw Ted standing by her station with her machine pumping out information as if it had a mind of its own. She started running over toward it when I tackled her. Ted came over and extended a hand; she reached out for it, and he would have succeeded in pulling her up if I had not punched him in the stomach. He doubled over, clutching his stomach, and I sat down on the small of Murph's back. She started pounding her hands and her feet on the floor like a baby throwing a tantrum. Ted recovered enough to say, "Murph, get up this minute and go to your machine and shut it down."

She couldn't. I continued sitting on her, and when Ted made a move toward the computer terminal or toward helping Murph, I thwacked him behind the knees.

Murph stopped kicking and began praying, "Blessed Mary, Mother of God, please take this madness from me." That was one of her prayers. Another one, addressed to the same person, was to ". . . take this burden from me." I felt

85

sorry for Murph and would have asked Malcolm to hurry except that I knew that in his slow, methodical way, he was hurrying.

Ted was screaming orders, asking Ruth to get Washington on the phone and tell them to get their ass *down here* and asking Hazel to go to the electrician and tell him to get his ass *up here* and asking Lester to call IBM and tell them to get their ass *over here*. I thought it was interesting that the computer said please, but Ted did not.

In a deep, gruffy voice I said, "And call the exorcist to get his ass *inside here*." I had never dared to say *ass* in public before, never having been assigned reading from the part of the Bible where it is written.

Other operators began shutting down their stations to see if they could help, and I knew it was a question of time before Murph would be rescued. My weight could not withstand the force of several grown people pulling at her. Malcolm looked over his shoulder and saw what was happening, and called out, "Hold on tight, Jeanmarie. I'm almost finished." By the time he said that, people were so confused by what was going on that they paid little attention to a voice coming from the phantom at the computer.

Murph had stopped kicking and praying. She folded her arms in front of her and rested her chin on them and was lying there watching Ted get thwacked in the knees every time he approached her computer terminal. I think she was ready not to be rescued at all when two people lifted her under her arms, and two lifted her feet. They raised her up as if she were a stretcher, and unknown to them, they had managed to lift me, still seated on the small of her back, my feet dangling about two feet above the floor.

One of them asked, "Can you stand on your own two feet now, Murph?" And she replied, "I have this terrible weight on the small of my back. I've never had back problems before." Murph had not been lifted so high that I couldn't jump down, and I did. I moved over toward Malcolm because I saw that three men were coming to rescue the computer.

Malcolm seemed to have printed enough paper to make an encyclopedia, but he kept on typing. I had my work cut out for me. I ran toward one of the men and tripped him and made him fall. I reached Malcolm's chair just a second before the other two did. I reached in back of me and found a felt-tipped pen and began making jabbing motions with it, poking it right then left, then right again. The two men looked and marveled at this dancing pen. I felt like Wonder Woman. "The pen is mightier than the sword," I said in the same deep, gruffy voice I had used before. The men backed away and away until they turned tail and ran.

At that point, the entire office assembled in the far corner of the room. They linked arms and began moving toward us. I continued jabbing with the pen, and Malcolm continued pounding the keys of the computer. "We're doomed, Malcolm," I whispered. "Can you go any faster?"

"I'm almost done."

"Do you think eerie noises will help?"

"Try."

So I began to howl. I howled like a cat, and I bayed like a dog, and I mooed like a cow. The group continued moving toward us, slowly, slowly, arms linked, their eyes fixed like boiled eggs. Eerie noises helped convince them that we needed to be exorcised, and two of the women took tiny gold crosses from around their necks and pointed them toward the phantom computer.

"Are you finished?" I demanded of Malcolm.

By way of an answer, he said, "*Papillon!*" and we were pulled up toward the ceiling, a quire of paper floating after us like a poorly engineered kite. We touched down just outside the building, where both of us worked madly to gather all the papers together. I called, "*Papillon!*" once more, and we were zapped back through the Orgone before either of us had a chance to see if the outside of the Data Processing Center was very different from any of the other duck farms on Long Island.

🌿 🌿 🌿

MALCOLM proudly handed Tallulah the folded sheets of paper.

She pulled one end, and the paper began unfolding until it reached as high as her hand could hold it. She formed it into a half-circle and asked, "What is this, darling? Fan mail?"

"That's a computer print-out," Malcolm said.

She put on a pair of large, thick horn-rimmed glasses and began examining it closer. "Is it in English, darling?"

"Of course it is. What did you expect? Swahili?"

"I thought it might be in dashes and dots or glyphs. I never knew a machine that could speak English."

"It doesn't speak it," Malcolm said. "It writes it."

"It even says please," I added.

"Really?" We nodded. "I had no idea machines could be

so playful." She examined one of the pages. "Why, look at this. Edgar and Fiona Widdup own a nursery. They call it Smarty Plants." She put the papers down and removed her glasses. She thought a minute and said, "I like the name," thought a minute more and said, "sort of." She put her glasses back on and read some more. "They had a gross income of thirty-five thousand last year." She took her glasses off again before saying to Malcolm and me, "That's not bad." She put her glasses on and read some more, took them off and said, "You two better run along now. It's getting late." We started backing out, and Spot started following us. Without looking up from the sheets, Tallulah called him back.

Malcolm said, "We're going now, Tallulah."

"Ta-ta, darling."

"Don't you want to say anything to us?"

"See you tomorrow."

"Well, then, goodbye," Malcolm said.

"Ta-ta again." She looked up, took off her glasses and said, "You're waiting for me to thank you, aren't you?"

Malcolm shrugged. "You seem to be enjoying that stuff. I just thought you might like to take back what you said about computers and about mathematicians."

She said, "Take it back? But, of course, I do, darling. I had no idea computers wrote English. I adore the English language." She stuck the earpiece of her glasses in her mouth and saluted. "The last time Tallulah saluted was when the flag had forty-eight stars."

"That was before I was born," Malcolm said. "Long before."

"Yes, darling. You can use it as a measure of my compliment or as a measure of my age."

"I'll think about it," Malcolm replied.

"Tallulah has no doubt that you will." She put her glasses back on and started reading again, and we quietly exited downstage and through the Epigene.

Tallulah says, "*I have never spent a day in the country without wishing that Noah had not been so thorough.*"

eight

WHEN MALCOLM and I next arrived at Rahab Station, Tallulah was wearing her eyeglasses and reading the computer printouts. She had pushed half the pillows behind her so that she was sitting more upright than usual. Spot greeted us by bringing us a gift of the last sheet of paper, unfolding it as he dragged it across the room. "Oh, Spot," Tallulah scolded, "bring that back here." She took off her glasses and said to Malcolm, "This is fascinating, darling. I just adore its being written in English, but one has to turn it around every other page, doesn't one."

"You can tear the pages apart, Tallulah. You just break them apart at the folds." Malcolm sat on the floor and quietly rearranged the pages of the print-out. He also tore off all the edges.

"What are you going to do with all those strips from the

edges, darling. The holes are so even. They must be worth saving."

I said, "When I am rich and famous, and they have a Wall Street parade for me, everyone will throw confetti and those things at me. Save them for that."

"How do you intend to become rich and famous, darling?" she asked.

"By being wonderful."

"Darling, *I* was wonderful, but if they had a parade for me, I missed it. I think one must be in politics or be a hero to have a parade. Politics is simply out of the question, and being heroic seems so terribly physical. Tallulah never minded being brave, but she never enjoyed anything strenuous. I really don't care to walk on the moon. Really I don't. There's absolutely no one there to talk to—even *I* know there is no man in the moon—and I'm sure the food is just awful."

Malcolm said, "What I don't understand, Tallulah, is why you needed us to get these names and addresses. You knew where to send us during our trials."

"Yes, I did, didn't I, darling. My spirit has always felt close to poor old Mary Frances and dear old Horace, and I can always find them. But, you see, the awful truth is that my spirit is no longer in touch with any of the people who were there when I died. That is something that worries Tallulah a great deal; it is exactly what convinces her that one of them took her Regina Stone. But, now! Where would you like to start?" She put her glasses on again and began to leaf through the pages. "We have addresses for everyone but Emmagene."

"Yes, I know," Malcolm said. "I asked the computer for her forms three times, but nothing came up."

"Isn't it just awful that the computer knows our form? I never, I tell you, *never* told anyone my waist, hip or bra size. If they must look, they must estimate, I always say." She took her glasses off and asked Malcolm, "Does this mean that poor Emmagene's spirit has been sucked into all those vacuum tubes inside the computer, and the poor darling has lost her form?"

"Tallulah," Malcolm explained patiently, "I was asking for IRS forms. Income tax forms. Besides computers don't have vacuum tubes anymore; they have transistors."

"I guess it is very clever of them to have transistors, darling, but what does that mean for Emmagene Krebs?"

"What it probably means is that she hasn't filed an income tax form or that she doesn't live in the part of the country that uses this data processing center."

"Where else is there?"

"There's Indiana, for example. Maybe Emmagene is filing her returns there. That's where she came from originally. There are also all those states west of the Mississippi."

Tallulah lifted her head and looked at Malcolm through half-opened eyes. "Everyone keeps telling me that those places exist, but I don't believe it. Really I don't. I have never met anyone going to one of those places. I only meet people who say they came from them. Now, tell Tallulah, have either of you ever met someone who said she was *going to* Kokomo, Indiana?" Both of us shook our heads. "You see! I'm sure it does not exist. If it ever did exist, the food must have been simply awful, and everyone left." She put her

93

glasses back on and read the print-out pages again. "How about Glen Cove?"

"Which one's in Glen Cove?" I asked. "Malcolm and I haven't had time to read it."

"Practice that line, darling," Tallulah said.

"What line?"

"*I haven't had time to read it.* You'll use it all of your adult life. Learn to make it sound convincing."

Malcolm said, "Who's in Glen Cove?"

"Nicolai Ion Simonescu."

Malcolm said, "I want to start with Widdup. Jeanmarie says that the butler did it."

"Fine," Tallulah said. "Topside to Smarty Plants."

❧ ❧ ❧

WE WERE in a greenhouse that was as long as a city block. Along the sides were platforms that held thousands of pots of chrysanthemums. White to cream to yellow and lavender to burgundy. The yellow ones had more different shapes than the others. Some had short stiff petals; others had shaggy petals that made the blossom look unkempt. I took a minute to stand at one end of the greenhouse and look over the field of mums. I breathed deeply. The smell was ripe, not sweet, as much like cabbages as roses.

Standing there, I was unaware of Malcolm and unaware of our mission until an old Dalmatian came over to where I was standing and began sniffing at me. "Nice, Spot," I said and reached down and petted him. He wagged his tail and licked my invisible hand. Malcolm came over and started petting him, too. The dog was old; I could see that there was a lot of gray in the black spots around his face. I said to Malcolm, "This must be the then Spot that was living with Tallulah when she died."

He nodded. "I guess you're right about the butler doing it. Widdup or Fiona must have taken The Regina Stone. How else could a butler and maid have paid for a business like this? This is hardly some tiny little florist shop. This looks like a big wholesale operation."

A plain-looking woman wearing a long, gray cardigan came into the greenhouse just then. She looked around and started walking slowly down the length of the greenhouse. She stopped to pick a dead leaf off one of the plants, saying, "Now, there, sweetie, you don't need to hold on to that any longer." She walked a little further and straightened one of the other pots and said, "Stand straight and tall, dearie, and give Mr. Sunshine a chance." She reset the small seeper hose on another plant saying, "A little thirsty, are we?" Then she looked up, saw Spot and said, "Oh, there you are, Spot. Come along now. Widdup and I are waiting. You know we can't leave you out here." She walked over to where Malcolm and I were standing, and Spot began to whimper. "Come along now, old fella," she said. "Widdup has made you a kidney pie. Come along." Spot kept looking back toward us and wouldn't budge. Malcolm and I started walking toward Fiona, and Spot followed.

"What's the matter, fella? You're not getting moon madness again, are you?"

Spot whimpered a reply.

Malcolm and I lagged behind and watched as they walked

toward a house, a rather plain one-story house. They walked into a back door and closed it before Malcolm and I could get there.

"Malcolm," I said, "I think this is as good a time as any to see if we can walk through doors."

"Of course we can walk through doors. We do it every day of the week."

"I mean through *closed* doors."

"I think it is just as much fun to slowly turn the handle on the door, then open it and walk through. As a matter of fact, I prefer doing it that way."

"Malcolm," I said. "I am interested in knowing the limits of our magic."

"Funny for you to say that."

"And why is that so funny?"

"It is funny because it is usually me who wants to define things."

"I just need to know the limits of the magic, that's all. Will you please walk through that door?"

"Ladies before gentlemen."

I was afraid of breaking my nose or otherwise maiming myself. I hate the word 'maim'; it is the second ugliest word in the English language. "Promise that you will say the password immediately if you see any blood?" I asked. Malcolm said he would. "And tell the plastic surgeon that I'll need rhinoplasty."

"How do you spell that?"

"Just say nose job. Can you say nose job?"

"I can even spell it."

I walked up to the door that Fiona had just closed and stood full-face about three feet in front of it when Malcolm

96

told me to be practical and to lead with my shoulder, the way the television cops do. I turned around so that I was sideways to the door, and I pushed against it with my shoulder, but I didn't get through. Braving my nose and a separated shoulder, I backed off from it, way off, in order to get a running start, when Malcolm went over to the door, quietly opened it and walked in. I watched the door swing shut and heard Fiona say, "Widdup, I keep telling you that you have to do something about that door." Then I heard a deadbolt slide into place.

So I was locked out, and Malcolm was locked in. He could have used his magic fingers to pull the deadbolt back and open the door for me, but either he did not think of doing so or didn't want to. I waited for what seemed like a very long time, and the door did not open.

If the fates or Malcolm close one door, find another. I started walking around the house, looking for a window that I could break and climb through—even if it meant getting cut and bloodied in the process, but I didn't have to. I found the front door was unlocked. I walked into the parlor and decided to wait there for a little while and let Malcolm worry about me. I saw a book on a table and sat down on the sofa and started to read. The book was *The Secret Life of Plants* by Peter Tompkins and Christopher Bird. It was a big book, four hundred and two pages, if you count the index. There was a place marker at the beginning of Chapter Two, "Plants Can Read Your Mind." Page seventeen. I smiled to myself. Tallulah had said to practice the line, *I haven't had time to read it.*

I spent a few minutes leafing through the book. Some of the other chapter titles were: "Plants Will Grow to Please

You," "The Mystery of Plant and Human Auras" and "Live Plants or Dead Planets." Most of it seemed to be saying that plants can feel pain and respond to kind words and beautiful music. A lot of the clones at school had begun giving their plants names like Ernest and Daphne and talking to and about them as if they were people. I was willing to bet that none of them had read the book, but they had caught on to the fad, the way they had started piercing a second hole in their ears.

I put the book down and looked around the room. There was a piano against the wall opposite the fireplace. On top of the piano was a picture of Tallulah, with her chin tucked down and looking up through half-closed eyes. Not very different from the way she looked now. I guessed that this must have been one of her publicity photos. Tallulah was not beautiful, but she was memorable. Those high arched eyebrows and those painted lips. It was too bad that a person could not hear her, for her voice, that low pebbly voice of hers, defined her more than anything else. I thought that anyone who had had the good luck to have seen her on stage probably carried away from the theater something they would remember always.

I was halfway to the kitchen before it occurred to me that someone who stole The Regina Stone would hardly keep a picture of the person they had stolen it from right on top of their piano. The top of the piano, after all, is usually reserved for royalty or grandchildren, whichever you happen to know better.

When I got to the kitchen, I saw Widdup feeding Tallulah's then Spot. He was sitting on the floor, picking up pieces of kidney pie and hand feeding them to the dog.

Every time Spot would take some, chew and swallow it, Widdup would say, "Good, doggie. Nice fella." Fiona was watching. "His appetite seems improved today, wouldn't you say?"

"Yes, much better, dear," Widdup replied.

The kitchen looked like an extension of the greenhouse. There were plants everywhere. Some were enormous. Not what you would call house plants at all. They looked like the picture in my fourth grade science book that showed the prehistoric forest that had become coal. Malcolm was standing behind one tree-sized plant, beating his chest. "Me, Tarzan. You, Jane," he said to me.

Widdup said, "What was that, dear? Did you say something?"

Fiona thought a minute and answered, "I don't believe I said anything. Of course, one can never be sure."

"Don't worry, love. You'll think of it later."

"It may have been *Ficus benjamina* again. I noticed that he seems restless this evening."

Widdup replied, "Could well be. Spot does not seem himself either. I could swear that he is seeing things this evening. Do you think it's possible that he's gotten his sight back?"

"Stranger things have been known to happen, haven't they, duck? I've noticed that *Mimosa pudica* has perked up a bit." She leaned over and whispered to Widdup, "Perhaps, she's come out of her doldrums. It doesn't pay to be as sensitive as she is."

"I would like to think so, love," Widdup whispered back as he continued feeding Spot the kidney pie. Spot was looking up at Malcolm and me between mouthfuls. At last he finished everything that had been in the bowl, and Fiona handed Widdup another bowl filled with plain water. Widdup held this under his chin until Spot drank a good bit, then he got up and went to the sink where he washed out both bowls.

The minute that his back was turned, Malcolm and I sprang into action. We began ruffling the leaves of all the large plants in the room. Widdup turned to face back into the room and saw the plants waving as if swept by gale force winds. "Are you sure that I bolted the door, Fiona?" he asked, as he sat down to read the paper.

"I'll check it," she said. When she saw that the door was still bolted shut, she explained, "I just think the plants are restless tonight."

Widdup resumed reading his paper.

Malcolm called out in a high pitched voice, "E-E-E-ED-GAR WIDDUP, E-E-E-ED-GAR WIDDUP..."

Widdup looked up and asked, "Was that you, Fiona?"

"No, dear," she replied. "I think it was *Ficus benjamina*. He does seem to require an awful lot of attention this evening."

"Well, what is it then, Ben?" Widdup asked, looking at the plant that Malcolm was standing behind.

"I am the spirit of Christmas past," Malcolm said, still using the high-pitched, whiney voice.

"Good grief, Fiona," Widdup said, "I'll bet Ben is going to scold us again for not using him as a Christmas tree."

"He bears a grudge, that one," Fiona said. "I thought we made him understand that we never cut down the trees that we decorate. We just rescue the ones that are left in the Kiwanis lot over there in Riverhead."

Malcolm was beginning to look confused, so I ruffled the

leaves of the plant they had called *Mimosa pudica*, and the minute I touched the leaves, they began to fold up. I pulled my hand away quickly but not before Fiona noticed. "I think Mimosa wants to say something, dear."

Speaking with a high squeaky voice I said, "Where is The Legina Stone?" (The name Mimosa sounded Japanese to me, so I did my best Japanese accent.)

Fiona said, "Mimosa wants to know where The Legina Stone is, ducks. You don't happen to know a stone by that name, do you?"

Widdup scratched his head. "I can't think of any."

Malcolm interrupted with his high-pitched windy voice, as if a monsoon had hit his wind pipe. "Where is Tallulah's Regina Stone."

Fiona said, "Funny that Ben should bring up Tallulah. I've been thinking of her all day today for some reason. And just look at Spot, will you?" At the mention of Tallulah's name, Spot got up from his place beside Widdup's chair and started circling as if he were trying to catch his tail.

Malcolm asked, "Where is The Regina Stone?"

Widdup answered, "I wish I knew, Ben. Fiona and I would like to know which one of those buskers took it." He looked at Fiona and asked, "Wouldn't we, dear?"

Fiona nodded.

Malcolm stopped trying to speak in a haunting way and asked straight out. "How were you two able to afford this nice house plus the greenhouses plus all these acres?"

"Why, Ben," Fiona said, "we thought you knew. Tallulah left us her apartment in the city. It was worth a half a million. We've just done very well. We love you, Ben, and will never sell you, but we've sold a lot of your cousins. But don't worry and lose all your leaves again, dearie. They all have good homes. People don't come to Smarty Plants to buy unless they guarantee our babies good homes."

Malcolm said, "Come on, Jeanmarie. They didn't take it. We better get back to Jericho Tel before we begin growing roots."

Fiona tilted her head and said, "Why are you calling Mimosa Jeanmarie, Ben? Is she undergoing a mutation?"

Malcolm said, "She's fine, Fiona. She's just having a little identity crisis."

"She's so shy, you know. I wondered if she was just trying out new names."

Widdup said, "She's beyond the age where she should be doing that, love. Mimosa here is as old as Ben."

I said, "Let's get out of here, Malcolm."

"Just a minute," he said. He went over to Spot and patted him. Spot turned over onto his back. Malcolm started giving his underside a good rub, but I said, "*Papillon!*," and we disappeared from Smarty Plants.

Tallulah says, "Never wear jewelry that spells something. The quality should tell you everything except the time."

nine

THERE WAS FROST on the ground when I started for school the next morning, so I wore my quilted vest. It was one that Mother had bought me in a Western Shop when we lived in Texas. She had appliqued and embroidered designs of mountains and a setting sun on the back, and on one half of the front she had embroidered a yellow rose of Texas, and on the other half, she had done an oil derrick in silver threads.

Malcolm was waiting for me when I came out of the trailer. He studied my vest but didn't say anything until we were a few feet from the bus stop. "Nice threads," he said. "Did you do it?" I told him that my mother had. "I didn't think you had. It's so neat. Turn around," he said. I did. "I like the sun."

"Don't you like the mountains?"

"Just because I said I like the sun doesn't mean that I don't like the mountains. I like the whole thing. All right?"

"All right," I said, and we boarded the bus.

That year no one at school wore anything but blue jeans. The fact that everyone wore blue jeans did not make it any easier to know what to wear. It was important that your blue jeans have the proper drop waist and bell bottoms. And it was necessary that they look as if they had been washed a lot. Worn and faded was the order of the day for the jeans, and worn and tie-dyed was the order of the day for tops. I heard one clone brag that she didn't own a dress and another say that her mother wouldn't sit near her in church because she had insisted on wearing an unironed blouse. What would have been really different that year would have been for a clone to show up at church in a dress, one that was ironed. The girl clones at Singer Grove were just like the ones in Texas; they knocked themselves out to be like everyone else and then bragged about how they were different. All their differences put into a pot and boiled down wouldn't spice baby food. By trying to brag about how different they were, they just really showed how alike they were, because all their differences were alike.

The boy clones bragged about not being into clothes, but no one can wear clothes without being into them, and I saw two of them standing in front of a shoe store with their faces pressed against the window looking at boots with two-inch heels.

No one in all of Singer Grove Middle School had a vest like mine. It was authentic western wear, made into a work of art by my mother.

As I boarded the bus with Malcolm, I saw several of the

clones looking me over, but they said nothing. I figured that they were as jealous of me as Joseph's brothers were jealous of his cloak of many colors. School started, and I put the vest in my locker and forgot about it until I had to put it on to go home.

I still rushed to get on the school bus after school. I was less worried about becoming sick, but I was eager to get home to dump my books and go to Jericho Tel. I was sitting in the first seat behind the driver, bending over tying my shoe when two of the clones from my class got on. One of them was saying, "Her hair looks like it was cut with a lawn mower." I recognized the voice of Lynette Hrivnak. The clone who was with her said, "And did you see that strange thing she wore today? I think she must shop for her clothes at Goodwill." Then they saw me tying my shoe and made exaggerated shushing sounds to each other before taking their usual places in the back of the bus. I heard them giggle.

I did not look up from fastening my shoe immediately. If only I were invisible, I thought, I would go to the back of the bus where they were sitting and tweak their noses, pull their hair, run my fingernails across their cheeks, tear their T-shirts, kick their ankles, bop their chins, bite their hands, sock them in their stomachs and leave without their knowing what had tweaked, pulled, scratched, bopped, torn, kicked, bit and socked them.

Leaning down had brought blood to my face, and rage had heated me up until I felt like a Franklin stove. I took the time to tie knots in my shoes, then took a deep breath and made a decision. Rather than pretending that I had not heard anything, I would look up and find the faces that belonged to those voices. I did that.

I stared at Lynette first until she felt my eyes on her. I said nothing. At first she arched her eyebrows and stared back; her fellow clone did the same. I continued to stare. Lynette looked away, and the other attempted to smile. But the attempt did not come off. Before she had a chance to look away, I smiled. I continued to smile at her until she looked away in confusion. And all the rest of the way to Empire Estates Mobile Home Park, I stared at those clones, and I smiled each time one of them dared to return my look. By the time I got off the bus at my stop, I was very glad that I was visible. And I was so satisfied with what I had done that I didn't even bother telling Malcolm.

🌿 🌿 🌿

"YOUR GARMENT is divine," Tallulah said by way of greeting. "Come closer, let me look at it. Yes, you should always dress to suit yourself, Jeanmarie. I have never been a fan of fashion but I am a devotee of style. Remember that, darling. Stars have style."

Stars have style. She knew! Tallulah knew that I was a future famous person. She knew that I was going to be a star.

I told Tallulah about how the clones had made fun of me on the bus and how I had stared them down. "They were jealous; I know they liked it," I said, "I could see it in their eyes, but they will never admit it."

"It wasn't your vest they were jealous of," Tallulah said. "They were jealous that you had the courage to wear something that was really different." She then dismissed the whole subject with a wave of her hand and by saying, "Really, darling, don't seek great reviews from small minds. They have neither the character nor the vocabulary for them."

Malcolm was becoming impatient, and he asked Tallulah where she would be sending us. She did not answer directly but said that she was very curious about Nicolai Ion Simonescu. His IRS form showed that his place of employment was Queens, and he was living in Glen Cove. "I guess he did not marry Emmagene after all," Tallulah said. "On the form where it says name of spouse, he has written Lucinda Wells. He also has a total of four dependents including himself." She continued reading from the form, "Two children, Samuel and Amy Elizabeth. His place of business is called Nick's Novelties. I don't like the name. He was such a talented young man. Judging from his income tax return, Nick's Novelties is a success. Tallulah wonders what Nick's Novelties does. I guess he is not a ventriloquist any longer. I simply adored Anna Karenina. Adored her, I tell you. Let Tallulah do one of Nicolai Ion's routines for you."

She rearranged the pillows from her divan so that they propped her upright. She spread her legs as if she were holding a cello between her knees or holding a dummy on one of them. She started to speak and then stopped. "I forgot to describe Anna Karenina. She is dressed in a white satin gown, and she wears long white gloves and a tiara. Nicolai begins by telling his audience that Anna Karenina has been living in a far corner of Russia and does not know that Russia no longer has a czar. *Czar* is Russian for king, darlings. You ought to know what royalty calls itself."

"Were you royalty?" Malcolm asked.

"In my way, darling, I was. I ruled Broadway."

I had to ask Tallulah to continue telling us about Anna Karenina.

"Anna Karenina has been sent to the United States as the Russian ambassador to the United Nations, but, of course, she knows nothing of democracy and thinks that the United Nations is a large palace on the East River, and that everyone has been invited to a costume ball. That's the only way she can explain why the Arabs are dressed in burnooses, and the Africans are wearing dashikis, and the Indians have their heads wrapped in those divine turbans."

Then Tallulah really began. She spoke in two voices, one for Nicolai, and one for Anna Karenina. Anna's voice had a thick Russian accent. Nicolai asks Anna how she likes the United Nations.

ANNA: Is not bad, but I have make order for new furniture for the castle.

NICOLAI: What is wrong with the furniture you have now?

ANNA: Half of people make sleep at desks because they have not enough of bedrooms. I have order beds for guests to sleep.

NICOLAI: But, Mrs. Karenina, those people are not your house guests. They need desks, not beds. They are representatives of the world's nations. They are there to help all the countries in the world get along with each other.

ANNA: Cannot be possible. Is house party. They make only talk. Vairy much talk. Vairy much talk about money, vairy much talk about how expensive is everything.

NICOLAI: Yes, Mrs. Karenina. They are there to talk about the business of the nations.

ANNA: How can be business? Everybody say how poor he is. Just like big house party. Everybody dress up, everybody arrive in limousine, everybody kiss and shake hands in front and say terrible things in back, everybody talk, and nobody listen. Is house party, I tell you. Is house party.

NICOLAI: Tell me, Mrs. Karenina, what do you think of Leonid Brezhnev?

ANNA: Him, I nevair invite again. He look terrible in tuxedo, and when I ask him to clear up the table, he say that no, he not do, that *he* is head of party. I ask him what kind of party is that, and he tell me Communist Party.

NICOLAI: Yes, that is true. Leonid Brezhnev is head of the Communist Party. All of Russia is part of the Communist Party now.

ANNA: What they serve at thees party?

NICOLAI: No, Anna, everyone serves the party.

ANNA: You call me Anna. I call you Nicky. Now, tell me, Nicky, what you mean, everybody serve the party? How can be, everybody serving the party? Who are guests if everybody serve?

NICOLAI: Your whole country is now part of the Communist Party. No one is a guest, and no one is a host.

ANNA: Is no fun at such party.

Malcolm and I applauded. Without getting up from her lounge, Tallulah bent down from the waist and swept her arm along the floor and took a bow. She pulled her legs back up on the sofa, leaned back, lit a cigarette, blew out a puff of smoke and said, "Oh, he was a talented one all right, that Nicolai Ion. I wonder why he did not marry Emmagene, and I wonder if he took The Regina Stone."

Malcolm said, "We'll soon find out."

"Not today," Tallulah said. "Not today." She waved her hands impatiently. Malcolm and I stood there like two dummies, not knowing what to do until Spot came forward and started nudging us downstage. Tallulah seemed to be staring off into space; she seemed to have no interest at all in our presence. She looked down briefly and smiled at Spot until we stood directly under the Epigene. "Spot has given us the shaft," Malcolm said just as we were swept Topside and visible.

❦ ❦ ❦

THERE WAS no call for us on Saturday after Mother and I returned from our weekly round of laundry and shopping. There was no call for us all of that weekend nor on Monday and Tuesday of the following week. On Wednesday Malcolm and I ran all the way to Jericho Tel from the bus stop without even stopping at home to dump our books. Spot was not there. We walked away wondering if Tallulah had gotten mixed up with the change from Daylight Savings Time to Standard Time. She was very bad at numbers. Maybe she had set her clock back instead of forward. We discussed this possibility at length; we were hoping for an easy explanation. What we tried not thinking of was that Tallulah didn't want us: that either she did not want us to solve

110

the mystery of The Regina Stone, or she thought that we couldn't. Or worse, she just didn't want to see us anymore.

On Thursday, we decided to take our shovels to Jericho Tel. We had convinced ourselves that Tallulah wanted us, needed us, but that something had gone wrong with her or with the Epigene, and she couldn't reach us. We decided that it would be an act of kindness to break in. We stood together at the center of the Tel and pushed our shovels hard against the turf, but the minute the blades hit the dirt, they sent off sparks that spun us reeling back to the border of trees. Malcolm was dumped on one side of the weathergram tree, and I was on the other. It was not only our feelings that were hurt. We got the message: Appearances at Rahab Station were by invitation only. Tallulah didn't want us.

And on that day when sparks flew from our shovels, sparks flew between Malcolm and me.

It began with Malcolm saying that maybe all Tallulah had wanted from us was to locate the buskers. "The way I figure it, Tallulah is done with us."

"Done with us?" I said. "She can't be done with us, I am not done with her."

"That's an example of your illogical mind."

"But we have unfinished business. We haven't found The Regina Stone."

"Maybe it was never lost. Have you ever noticed that Tallulah never sends Spot Topside with his collar on. She never said those were all rhinestones. A dog collar full of rhinestones would be a logical place to hide a big diamond."

I said that I had noticed, but I had not put the two things together, and Malcolm said that he was not surprised that I had not, for it took a logical mind to figure out things like

111

that. Then he said that he didn't see how being invisible accomplished anything.

"You may be super logical, Malcolm, but there is something wrong with you if you think that everything has to accomplish something. If everything had to accomplish something, there wouldn't be any music."

"I can live without ever returning to Rahab Station," he said.

"Well, I can't."

"Don't be so dramatic. Of course, you can."

"I'm not finished."

"None of us is finished. No one is ever finished until he is dead."

"You're even wrong about that, logic-head. Tallulah is dead; you can look her up in the encyclopedia and see that she is dead, but she isn't finished."

"All I am saying is that she is finished with us."

"Well, don't say it because she isn't."

"Just because you don't want to believe it, doesn't make it true. The facts seem to bear me out."

I mimicked him. " 'The facts seem to bear me out.' You're so full of facts that I wonder why you don't franchise your brain to *The World Almanac.* 'The facts seem to bear me out.' "

"The fact is that I'm getting tired of being sent Topside to do her errands. I can live without ever being invisible again."

"Well, I can't," I screamed.

"Don't be so dramatic."

"Don't tell me not to be dramatic. Drama is my future."

He flicked his hands as if he were swatting an annoying

insect. "Well, it's not mine. Being invisible may help you, but it doesn't help me one little bit."

"Come to think of it, Malcolm, I don't know why Tallulah invited you into Rahab Station at all."

"She let me into Rahab Station because she needed someone who had some sense and who could be orderly and methodical about doing her errands."

"Orderly and methodical! Hunh! Who left his hand in his pocket? Not me. Not me."

"Who got the information from the IRS? That's the kind of orderly and methodical that you could never do, will never do, will never be able to do and neither could Tallulah, and I'll tell you why. Because you can't think straight, and neither can she. She may have invited you because of what she can do for you—give you hints about being a lah-de-dah actress—but she invited me for my brain. It's as simple as that. I don't need Tallulah, and I don't need Jericho Tel, and I don't care if we never get back to Rahab Station."

"You do, too, need Tallulah."

"Give me one good reason."

"I can't think of one."

He crossed his arms across his chest and smirked. "See? You can't think of one, and do you want to know why? Because you can't think. Period. That's your biggest problem, Jeanmarie. You can't think."

"I can, too, think. I can think that you are far from perfect, Malcolm Soo . . ."

"So what?" he said, looking down his nose and tightening his mouth. "No one is perfect. But my being imperfect has nothing at all to do with Tallulah."

"Oh, yes it does."

"What?"

"I don't know. But I know it does."

Now he mimicked me. " 'I don't know, but I know.' That's just like you, Jeanmarie. You know everything you don't know. How can you know without reasons?"

"I know a lot. I know you should have been nicer to Tallulah and lighted her cigarettes."

"I know she shouldn't smoke."

I said that he had no feelings, and he said that I had no sense.

I said he was constipated, and he said that I was a slob.

I said that he had the soul of a transistor, but he did not hear that because by then he had stormed out of Jericho Tel and left me hollering to the circle of pines.

❦ ❦ ❦

THE NEXT MORNING I wanted to miss Malcolm, so I waited until the last possible minute to leave for the bus. Malcolm must have had the same idea, for he was where he always was when I opened the door to our trailer. He looked the other way when he saw me, and I slowed up so that he could get well in front of me. He took a seat in the back of the bus, and I took my usual place behind the driver.

We pretty much repeated the process in reverse when we were let off after school. At home, I kept poking my head out the door of our trailer so that I would be able to spot Malcolm leaving his. When I didn't see him leave for twenty minutes, I decided to head out, and I did. He again had the same idea, for he was coming down the step from his trailer just as I reached it. This time, he slowed down, and I walked ahead to Jericho Tel, walked around the circle of trees to the opening and walked all the way in to the center to make certain that I had not missed Spot in the dying light of the late afternoon.

There was no Spot, and I passed Malcolm walking into the Tel as I walked out. I thought of telling him that it was not logical for a person who cared nothing about returning to Rahab Station to make a trip to the Tel. But I didn't say anything, and he didn't either, even though our shoulders almost brushed at the entrance.

※ ※ ※

THAT EVENING, I got a phone call from Lynette Hrivnak, the queen of clones. She told me that she was calling to find out if I was going to Radio City Music Hall for the Christmas show. Every year, Mrs. Spurling, the music teacher, bought fifty tickets and took a group of students to see it. The group would be going on the Saturday after Thanksgiving, and Mrs. Hrivnak, her mother, would be a chaperone, and that was why she was helping with the phone calls. They wanted to know if I would come. The total cost for transportation, box-lunch and show was twelve-fifty.

I wanted to go. I had been wanting to get to Manhattan; and since I had met Tallulah, I had been wanting to get there passionately. But I was worried that my stomach would let me down during such a long bus ride. When I did not say yes immediately, Lynette said that there was a fund to help anyone who couldn't afford it.

Who did she think she was to offer me charity?

Who did she think I was that I would accept it?

I got furious. I told her that I would be happy to buy a ticket. Then in a voice as sweet as the wind off a field of thyme, I said, "Maybe you have a little brother or some relative who is as tone deaf as you are, Lynette. I would like you to give him my ticket, darling. I really have never considered what they play at Radio City Music Hall to be music, and I have never thought what the Rockettes do can be called dancing. I thank you very much for asking me, darling, but please tell Mrs. Spurling and your dear Mama that I couldn't possibly attend." I said miMAH for Mama.

I hung up, and I was miserable. I knew that Lynette would waste no time in telling her miMAH as well as Mrs. Spurling what I had said. And Mrs. Spurling was the last person that I wanted to antagonize. Because of my visits to Rahab Station, I had decided to try out for a part in the spring production of *Rumpelstiltskin*.

If only Tallulah would send me Topside to Singer Grove Middle School, I could haunt Mrs. Spurling, and she would give me a part in *Rumpelstiltskin*. If only she would let me haunt Lynette Hrivnak so that she would throw up on the bus all the way to Radio City Music Hall and splash all over her chaperonish mother, which would be disgusting and make three other kids throw up, which would make them stop the bus in the tunnel leading to Manhattan, which would make the smell of vomit and car fumes so awful that all the girls would throw up. All the girls plus Malcolm. Which would make such a terrific traffic jam in the tunnel that they would miss the show at Radio City Music Hall, which would make the police arrest them for holding up traffic, which would make them spend the night in jail with whores and pimps and drunks who threw up.

But I knew Tallulah never would, and not because she was selfish. Deep in my heart, I knew that deep in her heart, Tallulah had other reasons for making Malcolm and me invisible. Being invisible had started something inside us. I decided that Malcolm was not comfortable with his invisible self, and I was. Maybe it was not Tallulah that Malcolm was mad at. Maybe Malcolm did not like what he saw when he was invisible.

But we made such a terrific team. Just as Tallulah had missed the *us* of the buskers, I missed the *us* of Malcolm and me. Missing the us of Malcolm and me was like a tragic disease. I developed symptoms of the common cold.

Tallulah says, "*I have never understood why people who have knocked themselves out to become stars, afterwards knock themselves out to prove they're just folks.*"

ten

MOTHER AND I had to eat Thanksgiving dinner at eleven o'clock in the morning because she was scheduled to report to the airport at three. We didn't bake a whole turkey, just the breast; we stuffed it with Pepperidge Farm corn bread stuffing mix and opened cans of sweet potatoes and Ocean Spray cranberry sauce; Mother and I prefer the jellied kind. We decided that we needed something green so we had some Niblets peas; the boiled-in-the-bag ones taste as good as fresh. I had intended to invite Malcolm and Mr. Soo so that they could have a true American Thanksgiving dinner, but I would have had to talk to Malcolm to invite them, so I didn't. "Let them eat tofu," I said.

Mother got dressed in her uniform immediately after eating and left for the airport because she worried that traffic would be awful. I felt restless and annoyed and wandered outside. I was walking aimlessly around Empire Estates when I found a dead duckling. Wild ducks sometimes swept down from the skies and mated with the ducks that the farmers raised. Unless someone took pity on the half-breeds, they were destroyed. You couldn't sell a duckling as Long Island duck if only half of it was. This one must have been raised as a pet, for it looked full grown to me. It probably got killed on its first solo flight. The poor thing was mangled and bloody. Half-wild is a dangerous thing to be.

I stood over the dead duck with my hands in my vest pockets, not wanting to touch and not willing not to. I wished Malcolm would walk by as he had when I had found the blue jay. I would be willing to bury the hatchet if he would be willing to bury the bird. I waited around, my hands clenched inside the pockets of my vest, waiting for Malcolm to appear by magic, but he was nowhere in sight. I would have to do it myself. With the edge of my boot, I gently shoved the carcass off the path and went home for the funeral equipment. Once inside, I wiped my boots with pine oil and washed my hands with Fels Naphtha soap before opening the drawer that held the aluminum foil. I found the calligraphy pen and ink and tore a strip of paper from a brown paper bag. I would do it; I would do it all and all by myself and hope I didn't end up in the hospital with salmonella from undercooked duck.

I picked up the shovel that was leaning against the back of our trailer, and I carried the duck at arm's length on the blade of the shovel to Jericho Tel.

I chose a spot near the ring of evergreens that bordered the Tel and struck the ground with the shovel, hoping against hope that the ground would yield and that I would find myself floating in the lavender light of the Epigene. I had to push hard against the edge of the shovel blade, for the nights had been cold, and the ground was frozen. The earth did not open up for me, and I had to scoop out the small grave, one shallow layer at a time. After I put the duck into the earth, I backed away, the way that Malcolm and I always had, and I sat under the tree where I would hang the weathergram.

I wrote: *Wild duck + sitting duck = dead duck.* Direct and to the point. My writing was not as beautiful as Malcolm's, but the vertical and horizontal strokes of my + were the same thickness. I hung the weathergram on the pine tree, and when I did, I found a small shred of one of our other weathergrams. I didn't know which one it was; the only letter I could make out was a small *s*, and one small letter *s* isn't much of a message.

I went home and took an entire bath with Fels Naphtha soap to wash off the salmonella, any possible psitticossis or botulism, which I intended to look up in Dr. Maceo E. Patterson's Encyclopedia as soon as I had finished my bath.

❦ ❦ ❦

MOTHER had Friday off. She had brought home a *New York Times* that someone had left in one of the waiting lounges at the airport, and I found that the Bleecker St. Cinema was having a revival of the movie *Vixen!*, starring Tallulah. I insisted that Mother take me. Beg as she would that she was tired and that she didn't want to drive all that distance just to see a thirty-year-old movie, plead as she would that I would get carsick on the long ride into Manhattan, I insisted.

I thought of telling her that it was a school assignment, but I didn't. I thought of playing on her guilt at leaving me alone for all of those latchkey hours, but I didn't. I was polite but firm, and she realized that I meant business and gave in.

We set out for Greenwich Village in the early afternoon. Mother parked the car at Shea Stadium; we took the subway and had to transfer to the E Train at Penn Station. We got out at Fifty-third and Fifth Avenue and then had to come above ground from a station that was at least three levels deeper than Rahab and take a bus down Fifth Avenue. The day after Thanksgiving is the busiest shopping day of the year, and everything about the sidewalks of New York seemed to bear that out, but the more complicated and crowded the going became, the more determined I became to see *Vixen!*

I thought that Mother and I would be two of about six, possibly eight, people who were interested in seeing Tallulah. Actually, since Mother wasn't interested, I thought that I would be one of about six, possibly eight people, but I was wrong. The movie was full.

On the screen Tallulah looked just as she did in Rahab Station. She had the same painted mouth. You could tell that it was lipstick even though the movie was in black and white, and when the camera came in close up, you could see the false eyelashes, and her fingernails were the same ten wonders of the modern world.

She played a young girl who works in a department store and who marries the son of the owner, even though his mother hates her because she thinks Tallulah is not good enough for her son. The son turns out to be a drunken bum who fools around with other girls behind her back and

121

causes all kinds of trouble in the store because he neglects business as well as his loving wife. Tallulah saves the family business and lets the mother think it was her son who did. The son appears at his mother's deathbed and realizes that his wife has never told his mother how disgusting he was; he doesn't tell her either. Instead, he gives up drink and other women and returns to Tallulah, and they end with a kiss. Her lipstick didn't smear.

It was a good story. Mother cried. I cried, too, but not as much. I didn't ask her if she was glad she came because I knew that she was. We came out of the movie crying but smiling, and I asked her if she would like to see Washington Square Park since we were in the neighborhood. She suggested that we get some take-out pizza and eat it in the park. And we did that.

We found a bench with a clear view of a juggler who was tossing grapefruits, oranges and Brazil nuts in the air so fast that they looked like fruit salad. He finished his act, and the crowd thinned out just before he passed his hat. After the juggler left, a sidewalk stand-up comic appeared, clapped his hands for attention and then began insulting the hecklers who had answers for questions he had not asked. Some people left, but others came.

One of the problems of living with my mother was that we lived so close together in our trailer, and so much of our time together put me into the role of daughter and her into the role of mother, that I almost never saw her from the audience. Once in a while, when we were removed from the home ground, she would give me some hint about her other life, and she did that now. "I love a city," she said. When I mentioned that the crowd seemed to change as the acts did, she sighed contentedly and said, "I guess that is what is meant by panorama—the whole scene changing time after time." She took a large bite of pizza and chewed it, watching the panorama. "Nice place to visit," she said, looking at me and laughing. "People always say that about a city. 'Nice place to visit, but I wouldn't want to live there.' I would. I would want to live here. But I would also want to be very, very rich." She crunched up all the wrappings from our pizza but made no effort to deposit them in the trash container. She leaned back against the bench and put her hands in her coat pockets and let the crumpled ball of paper sit on her stomach. "Just look at them," she said. "If the animals you love best in this world are human beings, then the city is the place to be. It will show you every variety. Look at that woman waiting over there. She looks like someone left over from another century."

The woman who had caught Mother's eye was wearing a long calico skirt. On her head was a black felt bonnet with three strange looking feathers tucked into its band. The hat tied under her chin, and a fringe of golden-brown ringlets poked out from under it. One of her hands was holding an old wicker basket, and the other was pulling on a long cape, in order to clutch it tighter around her neck. She looked like an old-fashioned illustration of Little Red Riding Hood done before color printing was invented. She caught my eye and smiled at me in the hesitant way a person smiles at someone known in one place but seen in another—like meeting the girl from the supermarket checkout counter at the dentist's—showing dimples that added a sweetness to the old-fashioned prettiness of her looks. She lifted the basket she was carrying in a kind of salute. Her gloves were a rough gray wool, and the tips of two fingers were worn through. I studied the feathers in her bonnet; like a friend's handwriting, they looked familiar but they took a minute to identify. They were the feathers of a half-wild duck.

Mother said we better leave and got up, deposited our trash in a container and looked around, expecting to find me still at her side, but I had remained on the bench. She came over and began tugging on the lapel of my coat. "C'mon, Jeanmarie," she said, "it's a long way home." I didn't budge. "What's the matter?" she asked. "You look like you've just seen a ghost."

I didn't tell Mother that I had.

I had just seen Emmagene Krebs.

Tallulah says, "*The telephone and the light bulb were invented by men who knew how to make them work but didn't know why. That's the way people should raise children.*"

eleven

MOTHER AND I both slept late the next morning. It was the Saturday that everyone, including Malcolm Soo, was going to Radio City Music Hall. I first wakened about eight and thought about going to Malcolm's to tell him about having seen Emmagene Krebs. That would lead to his asking me how I knew that it was Emmagene, and that would lead to my telling him that I didn't have her finger-prints, but I knew it was Emmagene as surely as I knew that I was Jeanmarie, and that would lead to his telling me that if I were as smart as I was certain, I would be Einstein. There was an even stronger possibility that I would talk and he wouldn't answer, that he would just walk away, so I turned over and went back to sleep. It was ten o'clock when I woke again. Mother was already dressed, ready to go grocery shopping. I told her that I wanted to skip doing groceries and laundry, that I was too tired from yesterday.

Which was not exactly the best thing I could have said. Mother was also tired. She had had to do all the driving and all the asking for directions. She had to get the groceries today, and she would have to go to work tomorrow. I was glad I had not laid a guilt trip on her yesterday when I had been tempted to. I was sorry that I would not be helping her with the groceries and the laundry, but I knew it was time for me to return to Jericho Tel. I had to make another withdrawal from my good-daughter account.

¥ ¥ ¥

I WAITED only long enough to know that Mother's car would have cleared the trailer park before I headed out to Jericho Tel. As soon as my feet hit the opening to the clearing, I peered into the center to see Spot. He was not there. I decided to walk toward center anyway and saw a glowing white outline in the shape of a dog appear. Next the dog's eyes became three dimensional, and the dog looked at me. Within only a second, the entire dog came into focus, spots and all.

It was Spot.

Except it wasn't. He was the same and different. Could Spot have changed his spots?

Suddenly I knew. This was Tallulah's Then Spot, the dog that Malcolm and I had met at Smarty Plants. I called him to me. He cocked his head slightly to one side. I called again, and he came bounding over to me and began licking my face. Yes, this was Then Spot, for he was much friendlier than Now Spot. I walked to the center of the Tel, and he followed me. I wiped his licks from my face with a piece of Kleenex. It occurred to me to test something, so I rolled the tissue up into a ball and threw it toward the weathergram tree. Spot went for it. His sight had been returned.

I was so glad for him and so happy to know that in a few seconds I would be back in Rahab Station that I laughed out loud. Then Spot returned to me, carrying the wad of Kleenex in his mouth. I patted him and hugged him and would have kissed him had I known that it was medically safer to kiss a dog than to kiss a human. I tapped the ground three times, and the two of us were whooshed down off the face of the earth and into the Epigene.

Tallulah was lying across her satin sofa with Now Spot sitting on the floor with his head stretched up, resting on a mauve pillow near her elbow. She greeted me with a question. "How did Spot do, darling?"

"He was fine, Tallulah. I watched him incorporate."

"Really, darling, I think you mean you watched him become corporeal. It was his first outing since he arrived." Then Spot loped over to the sofa and sat with his head resting on a cinnamon colored pillow near Tallulah's knee. Now Spot got up and tried to nudge Then Spot away. Tallulah watched the juggling for space and said, "It has been a problem, darling. My Now Spot has suffered terribly from jealousy." She looked at him and said, "Haven't you, darling?" Now Spot began to whimper. "Neither one of them would give up the name Spot, and it has been exhausting. I tried calling them Number One and Number Two, but they would not respond at all to those names. I can't say that I blame them. Who wants to be called by a bathroom function? My first Spot had completed his half life and had gone onto his true afterlife before my second Spot arrived at Rahab. I had hoped that the same thing would happen before my third Spot arrived, but it didn't." She shifted herself around so that she was lying in the opposite direction of the sofa. "I only know that calling all my Dalmatians Spot may have made my life on earth easier, but it has been hell these past couple of weeks. Well, maybe not hell—that is an entirely different place—but I can tell you it has not been easy. Talk about sibling rivalry! No, don't."

"Don't what?"

"Don't talk about sibling rivalry."

"I can't talk about sibling rivalry. I have no sibling."

"Be thankful that you haven't, darling. You are probably a much better conversationalist for not having any brothers or sisters. Very dull topic, sibling rivalry. They all say the same thing: 'Mother loved you best.' Very whiney." She looked around.

I thought she was looking for Malcolm, so I told her where he had gone.

"Imagine someone paying to see the Rockettes. It is rather like paying to watch someone stir soup."

I tried not to smile. "Are you going to send me Topside?" I asked.

She pulled the sheets of the computer print-out from behind one of her satin pillows. They were all crumpled and stained. I asked her what had happened. "Darling," she explained, "Then Spot became infantile about some of his habits. Tallulah has felt like a zoo keeper." She put a cigarette into a holder and held her match ready to light it, stopped, blew the match out and said, "Tallulah has always loved her Spots, but she is not an animal lover." She struck another match while she held the cigarette holder between her lips. "I'm happy to see you again."

"Thank you," I said. "I'm happy to be back."

"Shall we resume where we left off?"

"I would like to."

"I don't think that Nicolai Ion would be at work today, so I shall send you to his house in Glen Cove. Remember stage left and through the Orgone."

"And *Papillon!* when I want to return."

I started out of Rahab Station, and Then Spot started to follow me. Tallulah called him back, and I heard her lecturing him as I entered the Orgone for my first solo trip Topside.

⚜ ⚜ ⚜

I WAS IN an upstairs room in a large house. There was a sofa at one end of the room and a desk at the other. Bookshelves from floor to ceiling lined two of the walls. The side of the room that held the desk had a window over the desk and two filing cabinets on one side and three on the other. A man was sitting at the desk working on some papers. On top of the corner file cabinet to the right, propped between the wall and a beer stein full of Ticonderoga #2 pencils, sat a ventriloquist's dummy wearing a white satin dress, long gloves and a tiara. Anna Karenina. I would have known her anywhere.

Using the lowest handle of the file cabinet drawer as a step to give myself a boost, I climbed on top of the file cabinet and put Anna Karenina on my lap. The man at the desk was so busy writing things and doing arithmetic with the help of a small calculator that he didn't even notice that Anna had changed positions. I coughed. He looked up for only a second before resuming his figuring. I coughed again. This time he looked up and around, shook his head and returned to the work on his desk.

I sneezed twice before saying in a deep Russian accent like the one Tallulah had used when she had told Malcolm and me about Nicolai's routine, "You have too much of dust in my place, Nicky. Why you not dust me off?"

Without looking up, Nicolai replied, "I'm sorry, Anna, but there's so much work to do. I want to finish these estimates before Lucinda and the kids get home."

ME (as ANNA): Listen, Nicky, you have made neglect of me, Anna Karenina, for long time now.

NICOLAI: [*still without looking up*] I know, Anna, I know, but I have to make a living.

ANNA: Why you not make me a living, too, Nicolai? We had very much talent, together, you and me.

NICOLAI: [*looking up at last*] Yes, Anna, we did. But the problem was that we just didn't make it.

ANNA: What you mean, we not make it? What ees *it*?

NICOLAI: *It* is the big time, Anna. We just didn't make it.

ANNA: How can you say you not make it? You are a rich man, Nicolai Ion Simonescu. [*I moved Anna's hand as if she were checking her tiara*] Did you steal the crown jewels, Nicky?

130

NICOLAI: Hardly, Anna. Hardly that. It's more a question of selling the crown jewels.

ANNA: Listen, Nicolai, you not talk to me in a long time. A vairy long time. Longer than since you not dust me. You not really make talk with me since Tallulah go belly up. You make talk with me now, Nicky.

NICOLAI: [*He tossed his pencil across his desk and put his hands behind his head and leaned back in his swivel chair. He smiled, mumbled Tallulah, put his feet up on the desk and tilted back.*] Strange you should mention Tallulah, Anna. I've been thinking about her on and off all day. She always believed in our talent.

ANNA: Then why you not stick with Anna Karenina?

NICOLAI: I tried, Anna, I tried. Remember the winters when I had to set you on the shelf to entertain children at birthday parties just so I could make enough money to get us through the year? [*He stared out the window, said half to himself.*] I was so upset when I realized that these little kids, these pre-schoolers, didn't think my Anna was very funny. [*He looked again at Anna and smiled.*] That's when I made animal and monster puppets to entertain them just so I could earn enough money for us to continue with our act. We were so fine, Anna. So fine.

ANNA: Why you give up, Nicky?

NICOLAI: It takes more than talent, Anna. I didn't give up until after Tallulah died.

ANNA: Why you give up then, Nicky?

NICOLAI: Circumstances. Certain things came my way I

131

have always thought that Tallulah would understand. We had the talent, Anna, but we didn't get the breaks. Tallulah would understand that if the breaks don't happen one way, you have to make them happen another.

ANNA: So tell me, Nicky, what you do now?

NICOLAI: I am a businessman.

ANNA: What kind of business you make?

NICOLAI: I design and manufacture animal and monster puppets. Kids love my puppets. One of the birthday parties I didn't take you to was for the son of a television producer. He saw how much his kid loved my monster puppets, and he asked me to design and make some puppets for a children's television show. The children's show became popular. I bought a factory. My puppets are stars, Anna. Not you. Not me. Now I even sell licenses and franchises to people who want to use my puppet characters on coffee mugs or T-shirts. I am the puppet king of show business.

ANNA: I have hear about puppet kings, Nicky. What I have not hear about is Burger King. What kind of king is that?

NICOLAI: That is not a real king, Anna. Burger King is a fast food chain.

ANNA: I have hear of fasting. Mr. Mahatma Gandhi have very much of this fast. I have even hear of famine although in Russia it nevair happen. Or you fast, or you eat. Food cannot be fast, so how can it be, a fast food chain?

NICOLAI: No, no, Anna, this fast, does not mean "not eating." This "fast" refers to quick. Burger King is a quick

132

food chain. People who are in a hurry come in and order a hamburger and some potatoes. Sometimes they eat them standing up, sometimes they carry them out of the restaurant to eat in their offices.

ANNA: In Anna's castle, everyone, even Anna's peasants, eat sitting down. Only animals eat standing up.

NICOLAI: [*He took his feet off his desk and sat forward and put his hands over his face. He started to laugh.*] I keep forgetting where you came from, Anna.

ANNA: Do you miss me, Nicky?

NICOLAI: Miss you? Of course, I miss you, Anna. What I don't always remember is how much.

ANNA: *Vairy* much is how much you miss Anna Karenina. You get me new gown and new crown, and we go back on the street, Nicky baby.

NICOLAI: It's a date, Anna. Now, let me get these estimates done, and I promise you we will go busking just like old times. [*He leaned over his papers again.*]

ANNA: You make date with me, Nicky. I want to know when. Anna Karenina have need to know the date to make fit the palace schedule.

NICOLAI: [*Checked a calendar on his desk.*] December twenty-second, Midwinter's Night, looks good.

ANNA: What you mean, looks good? How can you tell from piece of paper what day will be like. It will be cold. Anna Karenina will need a cape. You must make Anna Karenina a cape with a fur lining. No fun fur, Nicky baby. Russian sable.

NICOLAI: Your wish is my command, Anna Karenina.

ANNA: One more thing, Nick. Since you have become rich man, have you seen the girl Emmagene?

NICOLAI: Emmagene. Sweet Emmagene. [*Gazed out the window.*] Emmagene Krebs. [*Looked back at Anna.*] I have not seen her in a long time. Right after Tallulah died, I asked her to marry me, but she refused. When I asked her why, she said that she had to be free when her big break came. I told her that I would not stand in her way, but she said that she had to seek her fortune before she had finished singing the eighteen thousand songs she had to sing. She disappeared from the streets and from my life. The spring after Tallulah died I heard that she was appearing at a coffee house in Greenwich Village. The next Saturday night I went there, but her show had closed just the week before. I asked around, but no one seemed to remember a lovely young woman with a pure and sweet voice. I looked for her for a long time, but then I stopped.

ANNA: Maybe Emmagene hide out under a Rolling Stone or maybe she become one of those singing Spiders, Nicky.

NICOLAI: They're Beatles, not Spiders, Anna. She's not a Beatle or a Rolling Stone or any star that I have ever heard of. After all these years, I wonder if she has any of her eighteen thousand songs left to sing.

ANNA: We go busking in the Greenwich Village, Nicky baby.

NICOLAI: Midwinter's Night. Eight o'clock. It's a date.

* * *

I heard a door open downstairs, and I jumped down from the file cabinet. I called, "*Papillon!*" and heard Nicolai say, "I keep forgetting that you speak French," before I felt myself in the Orgone.

❦ ❦ ❦

I TOLD Tallulah everything that I had done on my first solo mission Topside. I reconstructed the conversation that Anna Karenina had had with Nicolai Ion Simonescu, and she laughed at all my good lines and applauded when I was done. I took a bow, sweeping my arm along the floor as she had done. "He's rich," I said. "I don't know how he got the money to start his business, but he must have gotten it somewhere. His house is a castle that would make Anna Karenina feel comfortable. She's still wearing her crown. Come to think of it, he could have hidden The Regina Stone right there in Anna's crown. No one would think to look in a dummy's crown. I certainly didn't."

"But, darling, if he sold The Regina Stone, he would no longer have it, and it couldn't be in Anna's crown."

"But you could use a diamond that big to get a loan from the bank. You said it was worth as much as a house."

"But, darling, why would the bank loan money to someone who doesn't need it?"

"I think that it is bank policy to loan money only to people who have something that is worth as much or more than the loan they ask for."

"Tallulah draws the line at trying to understand business. It involves arithmetic, you know."

I told her then that anyone who was as good an actress as

she was, didn't need to understand business. I told her that I had cried at her movie. She asked which one, and I told her.

She said, "Yes, darling, I was fabulous. My leading man in that movie wanted to marry me."

"Did you marry him?"

Tallulah gave me a long, cold stare. "Of course not. He was not in love with me; he was in love with the part I played. I told him that I, Tallulah, was much more than the sum of my parts, and that was far more than he could handle."

I asked her if she ever did get married.

"Of course, darling. I was married—let me think—four times. Unless you insist on counting that tiny little marriage I had just after high school. Then you would have to say five. And if you insist on counting my two marriages to the same man as two, then you would have to say I was led to the altar six times, darling. Wretched phrase: *led to the altar*. Sounds so sacrificial, doesn't it?"

"Did you love your husbands?" I asked.

"Very much."

I asked her if there was one husband that she loved more than the others.

"I loved them all equally. It was the time that varied. I loved one for fourteen years and one for fourteen days—that little marriage I referred to earlier."

"Were you married to the man who gave you The Regina Stone?"

"No, darling, I wasn't. He wanted to marry me, of course. He told me that there was great chemistry between us. I told him that if he wanted great chemistry, he should woo

Madame Curie. I could do nothing to improve that man's vocabulary. Instead of telling me that I was alluring and glamorous, mysterious and enchanting, he insisted upon referring to me as his jolly good girl. I told him I was none of those four things. I was not his, not jolly, not good, and I certainly was no girl. Words do count. People live and die by them. Ask Patrick Henry."

"Patrick Henry Mermelstein?" I asked.

"We'll take him up next time." Now Spot began to whimper. Tallulah addressed him. "Yes, Spot," she said, "Tallulah will send you for them next time." She said to me. "I don't know when I'll be ready for you again, but keep checking the Tel. And bring Malcolm."

I didn't tell her that Malcolm and I had stopped speaking to each other; I knew that she knew. And I also knew that her remark that I should bring Malcolm was not as casual as she made it sound, and the fact that I knew had nothing at all to do with her performance. She was, after all, still a wonderful actress. My knowing had something to do with the magic that was between Tallulah and me, something to do with my kind of knowing that happened without thinking, the kind of knowing that Malcolm did not understand or trust.

Tallulah says, "*Always use good grammar. It's like wearing designer clothing. People may not like your style, but they will pay attention to the cut of your cloth.*"

twelve

I DECIDED there was only one way to approach Malcolm, and that was directly, without rehearsal. To do it as if I were an already famous person who found arguments not worth remembering. To do it without thinking, which is the way that Malcolm said I did everything anyway. So the next day, right after Mother left for work, I walked over to his trailer and knocked on the door as if I had as much right to do so as an Avon lady or insurance salesman.

Mr. Soo answered. I had not thought of that possibility, and I knew that if I let that stall me, all was lost. So I made myself as bold as I was when I was invisible, and I said that I had come to see Malcolm and would Mr. Soo please ask him to come to the door.

I paid no attention to the fact that Malcolm was in his

pajamas. I said, "Tallulah wants us at the Tel. I'll wait for you by the weathergram tree."

"Jericho Tel is not so large that you have to tell me exactly where you'll be. I could find you if you just said Jericho Tel. You don't have to say by the weathergram tree."

"You don't have to be didactic."

"You are being didactic when you say the weathergram tree at Jericho Tel. You are also being didactic when you use the word didactic."

"I'm glad you said that, Malcolm. For a minute I thought that I had missed you." I turned to leave.

Malcolm called to me. "Wait up. I have to make a phone call, and then I'll be right there."

I told him that he better get dressed, too, and he looked down at his pajamas and was not at all embarrassed by being in them. I sat down on the step to his trailer and waited, feeling glad that Malcolm would return to the Tel. He was certainly aggravating, but he did not make me mad the way the clones did. He made me mad, but in a different way. I was as different from Malcolm as I was from the clones, but his differences were interesting even though they were aggravating. We simply had a different way of looking at the world—both inside and out.

As soon as he came out, I asked him whom he had had to call. He said Lynette Hrivnak, and I think I snorted before I asked him why he had to call her. He said that she had asked everyone who had gone to Radio City Music Hall over to her house to listen to records. I told Malcolm that he would probably be back from the Tel in time to go, and he said that he would just as soon skip it, that he would rather go to the Tel.

"I suppose you loved the Rockettes," I said.

"I liked them for the first ten minutes or so. They did everything very precisely. Then I got bored. I thought it was a lot like coloring and staying inside the lines. Neat but not very imaginative."

"Malcolm Soo," I said, "I think there is hope for you after all. What did you have for Thanksgiving?"

"We went to my aunt's house in Elmhurst over in Queens. We always go to her place for the holidays."

"You have an aunt living in Queens?"

"Sure."

"Cousins, too?"

"Two. A boy and a girl."

"Why didn't you tell me?"

"You never asked."

"You always led me to believe that you were a half-orphan."

"I am. What does having an aunt have to do with being a half-orphan?"

"A lot. It has a lot to do with it."

"Name one thing."

"Not now."

" 'Not now' because you can't ever."

"I can, too. I just don't want to. I just can't believe that someone who has an aunt living in Elmhurst, Queens, would let someone invite him and his father to Thanksgiving Day dinner even though they already had an invitation."

"You seem to forget, Jeanmarie, that you never did invite me."

"But I would have. I was going to ask my mother to ask

you and your father. Now, I'm glad we didn't because you would have refused. Does your aunt live in a house?"

"Yeah."

"Does she live with her husband?"

"Yeah. He's my father's brother."

"I just think you ought to have told me about all those Soos. That's all. I just think that if I had an aunt and an uncle and a couple of cousins, I would have told you."

"I couldn't have told you. We weren't speaking to each other."

"You could have told me before we weren't speaking to each other."

"It never came up."

"Now you not only have an aunt and an uncle and one of each kind of cousin, you also have Lynette Hrivnak to visit. You are a social animal, Malcolm Soo. Like a termite."

"And you are jealous."

"I am not jealous. I may not have been as busy socially as you, but I have been busy."

So Malcolm and I spent our first day back together at the Tel, sitting over Rahab Station waiting for Spot to appear. It was a very full kind of waiting, for we had a lot of catching up to do. I told him about seeing Then Spot become corporeal right before my eyes, and I told him about my visit with Nicolai. I told him about seeing *Vixen!* with my mother, and I went through the whole plot of the movie with him. He loved it. He said, "She must be a pretty good actress to be able to play an innocent."

I shrugged. "Maybe when she played in *Vixen!*, she was innocent. She had only been married three times by then."

141

I told him about visiting with Nicolai Ion Simonescu at his house in Glen Cove, and Malcolm was interested in everything I had to say. He asked about Anna Karenina, and I repeated our conversation as best I could, which was pretty good, which, in fact, was perfect, except that I left out the part about making a date with Nicolai and Anna for Midwinter's Night, and for reasons already stated, I also left out the part about having seen Emmagene Krebs.

Malcolm asked what else I had done over Thanksgiving. I told him nothing else, but he insisted. "I know there is something else, Jeanmarie."

"How do you know?"

"There is a language other than words."

"Do you really believe that?"

"Yes." He scuffed the ground with the toe of his shoe. "Now I do. I think that passing through the Epigene has helped me to see the unseen. Don't get me wrong. I don't like the idea that there's more to life than its facts, but it seems that is a fact of life."

Malcolm had told me that a funny thing had happened to him on Thanksgiving day. It involved his cousin, Mildred Soo. The family was all sitting around the dining room table after having eaten, and Mildred had taken the wishbone and asked him if he would like to make a wish with it. Each of them rested one elbow on the table and held onto one end of the bone. Mildred told him to close his eyes and make a wish. He did. He opened his eyes and saw that Millie's were still closed. He waited, his elbow still resting on the table, and as he did, he heard her wish. Heard it inside his head. He quickly looked around the table and saw everyone smiling at them, their expressions unchanged. Millie had certainly said nothing out loud, but he knew that she had wished that someone named Robert would call. Millie opened her eyes, and they pulled on the wishbone, and Millie got the long half, and Malcolm said, "He'll call." And Robert did.

"Now I'll tell you what else," I said. "I saw Emmagene Krebs." And I described what I had seen at Washington Square Park.

Malcolm was silent a long time. He had picked up a twig and was drawing circles on the ground with it. "If Emmagene Krebs is still a poor busker, still singing out her eighteen thousand songs, then it doesn't seem likely that she took The Regina Stone. She would be as rich as Nicolai unless she is crazy like Widdup and Fiona. But, of course, she wouldn't be crazy like them. She could be *as* crazy, but she wouldn't be crazy in the same way."

I told Malcolm that I wasn't so sure that Fiona and Widdup were crazy, that I had seen a whole hardcover book written about talking to plants.

"But, Jeanmarie, their plants *answer*."

"You just said that there is a language other than words."

Malcolm rolled his eyes up to the sky. "Jeanmarie," he said. "Jeanmarie," he repeated.

"What?"

"Jeanmarie, just because I believe that robins sing, do I have to believe that they sing opera?"

"What are you trying to tell me?"

"I'm trying to tell you that you still have to deal with facts. You may not see the facts. You may not want to see them. But there are times when the facts are there and you have to find them and deal with them. And Widdup and Fiona

143

are crazy. They may be nice crazy, but one of the reasons that they are crazy is that they don't deal with the facts."

"What about being invisible?"

"I can deal with that. It is a fact. And being invisible has shown me that there are invisible facts."

"Are you talking about electricity and x rays?"

"No!" he said impatiently. Then he jammed his hands into his pockets. He thought a while before he added, "Maybe yes and no. I'm talking about invisible forces as real as x rays, *yes*, but not ones that can be measured, *no*. And you are quicker and probably better at seeing those forces than I am, and if there was anything I missed in the past few weeks it was seeing the unseen."

"Well, Malcolm Soo, if there was anything that I missed in the past few weeks, it was your pigheadedness."

"Thanks a lot."

"Pigs are supposed to be pretty smart, you know." That was the closest I would come to telling him that I had missed him. "I have something else to tell you," I confessed. Malcolm asked what it was, and finally I told him that I had made a date with Nicolai and Anna Karenina for Midwinter's Night in Washington Square.

Tallulah says, *"Actresses who take small sums posing nude for magazine centerfolds have little to show for it."*

thirteen

THE FIRST DAY back at school after Thanksgiving vacation is not like any other first day. It is the day that is a beginning only to mark an end. You no more than set your foot inside the door than you begin a countdown to Christmas. By the time Christmas recess begins, there is a kind of coming togetherness—between teachers and students and also between classes—that doesn't happen at any other time of year. That may partly account for the fact that I felt closer to Malcolm when we returned to school than I ever had before. Closer to him than I ever had to any other classmate. Maybe it was just that we had quarreled and made up, and scar tissue is tough. Maybe it was just that Malcolm had also missed the *us* of us, and even though he couldn't bring himself to say it, he allowed it to show.

On that first Monday after Thanksgiving when we got to

Jericho Tel. Now Spot was lying on his back, his four feet sticking up in the air, stiff as a frozen turkey. He was trying to out-perform Then Spot so that we would tell Tallulah how good he was. He played dead even after we tapped the ground, and he landed on top of the Epigene on his back. I was glad that he was not human or living, for he would have caused himself a spinal injury that could have resulted in serious permanent paralysis.

Then Spot sniffed Malcolm as if he were the corner of an unfamiliar building. After he had satisfied himself that Malcolm was a friend, he jumped up on him; his paws rested on Malcolm's shoulder, and he began licking his face. Malcolm did not seem to mind. For a neat person, Malcolm did not seem to worry about parasites very much. I came to the conclusion that neatness and cleanliness were like apples and pears: both may be fruit, but they don't naturally grow on the same tree.

Tallulah was lying on her back with one arm beneath her head and the other across her eyes. Her feet were propped up on about fourteen pillows, and her silver birdbath ashtray was overflowing. "Tallulah is exhausted," she said by way of greeting. "Spots, Now and Then, have been behaving like children. As soon as I sent Now Spot Topside, Then Spot began to whimper. There is nothing quite so unsatisfactory as a whimper; it is the unfairest sound. Tallulah has truly suffered."

Then Spot was covering Malcolm's face with doggy kisses; and I thought that was about as satisfying as breathing mud, but Malcolm seemed to find it pleasant. He certainly did nothing to stop him.

Tallulah told us that we better get Topside immediately.

146

She didn't tell us where we were going, didn't give us instructions, didn't get up and didn't have to. I knew that we were going to visit Patrick Henry Mermelstein.

☙ ☙ ☙

WE WERE IN a music store. Behind the counter was a young man who seemed to be too young to be as bald as he was. What hair he had was reddish gold. He wore steel-rimmed eyeglasses, a blue pullover sweater and jeans that had a soft, worn look. Malcolm and I had been deposited on a countertop just to the right of the front door. The store was large. There were record bins that were labeled CLASSICAL or HARD ROCK or R&B or C&W. Music was being piped throughout the store that I could recognize as CLASSICAL. The door opened, and in walked two teenagers dressed in jeans. Malcolm jumped down from the countertop, more excited than I had ever seen him before. I looked again at the customers. They were the cousins Soo. I knew it.

Patrick Henry told them hi, calling one Reuben and the other Mildred. They greeted him, calling him P.H. They walked to a room in the rear of the store beyond the sign that said EMPLOYEES ONLY. We followed them and watched as they hung up their jackets and hats and pulled a large cardboard carton out from under a table. We could see that the carton contained a top hat, a deck of cards, a stream of handkerchiefs all tied together and a lot of other equipment that a magician might need. As soon as Patrick Henry came into the back room, Reuben left and went up front to mind the store.

Malcolm and I silently waited in a corner as we watched

Patrick Henry Mermelstein give Mildred Soo magic lessons. They were working on card tricks. P.H. said to Mildred, "Pick a card," and she did, and when he was halfway through the trick, Millie said, "I saw that." Patrick Henry told her that of course she did, that if she had not seen it, he would have been a good magician and a terrible teacher.

"What you have and I don't, Mildred, is talent," he said. "It takes more than practice to be a star. It also takes talent."

"What do you think of Doug Henning?" Millie asked.

"It's hard for me to say. I've only seen him on TV. I only trust live magic. When I see a magician performing before a camera, I always wonder how much is done with camera angles and special effects."

They worked for a while longer as Malcolm and I sat fascinated and silent. Millie did everything easily and very often perfectly on her first try. Watching Patrick Henry trying to do a trick was like watching an expert typist use a typewriter with the Russian alphabet: he knew all the moves but was puzzled that the finished product looked so strange. Malcolm moved closer to the table and invisibly and smoothly moved the cards and coins in the correct direction so that there were no spills and everything came out fine.

"You seem to be doing everything right, today. Don't you miss performing, P.H.?" Millie said.

"I do, Millie, I do." He leaned back in his chair and looked up at the ceiling. "Reuben's playing *The Carnival of the Animals*," he said absentmindedly. He tilted his chair back and continued staring at the ceiling. "I never made it. No one would hire me. I tried out for a small nightclub once, and the manager told me that I couldn't make chalk disappear with an eraser, but I kept going to auditions. The heck of it was, I didn't know that I was incompetent. I tried to make a living as a sidewalk vaudevillian. During the Christmas season, I helped out in my uncle's music shop. One evening after the Christmas rush was over, we closed the shop, and my uncle brought out a flute in a worn leather case and began playing. He was awful. I listened for a while and then said, 'I think you need some practice, Uncle. You've gotten rusty.' He replied, 'Rust has nothing to do with it. It is not practice that is missing. It is talent.' I knew that he was telling me something, but I was not ready to give up yet. A person who has talent has to believe in it, and a person who has no talent has to believe it. Then something happened that convinced me to give up."

Patrick Henry let his chair fall forward. He took off his glasses and rubbed his eyes. He lay his glasses down on the table and continued, "There were three of us buskers who used to pal around together, and we became friends with an old actress by the name of Tallulah. There was a ventriloquist, a singer by the name of Emmagene Krebs and me. Emmagene sang folk songs on the street. She had a sweet, untrained voice—genuine talent. She always said that she had eighteen thousand songs to sing. She kept count of how many she had sung and how many she had left. Then one Twelfth-Night, we were having a party at Tallulah's, as we did every year, and Tallulah died. Heart attack. No wonder, she smoked more than she ate. Emmagene became terribly upset, slightly hysterical, I'd say. She said that all of us were doomed to die as buskers, and only a handful of people would have heard her songs. She ran out of the house and disappeared. I guess that Tallulah's death had reminded all of us that we all have only eighteen thousand songs to sing, and my uncle's flute had reminded me that it takes more than practice to become a star."

Millie said, "I would like to do a live performance, P.H. Let's go out on the street."

"Are you crazy? I can't take time off from the shop. I promised myself when I opened this store that I would be a good businessman. My busiest season has just started." He wiped his glasses and put them back on. He shook his head. "Funny, I haven't thought about Tallulah in years. I haven't seen Nicolai—he's the ventriloquist friend I mentioned—in about four years. I got an announcement of the birth of his second child. I sent a Brahms recording, and I got a sweet thank you note from his wife, but I haven't seen the kid yet. I'll bet she's three years old by now."

I had been so interested in the magic and the conversation that I had not noticed when Malcolm left the back room. Suddenly, the music that had been playing over the intercom stopped. I heard someone clearing his throat. I knew where Malcolm was. I sat quietly and invisibly and awaited further announcements. I had a pretty good idea what they would be.

Malcolm's voice came booming out from the speaker. "NOW HEAR THIS. NOW HEAR THIS." Patrick Henry Mermelstein and Mildred Soo jumped. Before they could say anything, Malcolm bellowed into the microphone, "You, Patrick Henry Mermelstein will appear at Washington Square in Greenwich Village on Midwinter's Night, the twenty-second of December, and present magic to the people assembled there. Curtain up at eight P.M., P.H."

Patrick Henry Mermelstein slammed his hands down on the table and sent cards and coins quivering to the floor. He ran to the front of the store. Reuben Soo was running from the front of the store to the back. The two of them collided. "Why did you say that?" they asked one another. They both denied saying anything and headed back to the room where Millie was picking up the cards.

"Don't you have enough to do at the front of the store without interrupting my magic lesson?" she asked her brother.

"That was not me," he said. "Have you been learning to throw your voice?"

She stood up. "If I were, would I want to sound like that?" she asked.

"Like what?"

"Like Malcolm."

Malcolm snorted into the intercom. "Mildred Vivian Soo, what is your problem with Malcolm?"

Millie looked scared. "No problem. I promise you, no problem."

"Then why, Mildred Vivian Soo, do you not want to sound like Malcolm?"

"I wouldn't mind sounding like him. Really, I wouldn't."

"Yes, you would. Say why, or you will grow fat and your hair will fall out."

"Because h-e-e-e doesn't be-be-believe in magic."

Malcolm waited a long time before he answered. "Do you believe in it, Mildred Vivian Soo?"

151

"Y-e-e-e-s-s-s," she stammered.

"If you really do, Mildred Vivian Soo, why are you so frightened now?"

Mildred squared her shoulders, swallowed hard and said, "I am not frightened. I am just surprised."

Malcolm said, "Good. Then persuade Patrick Henry Mermelstein to be in Washington Square Park on Midwinter's Night at eight o'clock."

"Do you want me there, too?"

"No. You and Reuben are to watch the store while P.H. goes busking."

"Yes, sir," Millie said.

"And you're to do a good job of it."

"Yes, sir."

"And next Thanksgiving, you're to help with the dishes."

"It wasn't my fault. I got a phone call."

"Next time you'll help."

"I *told* you I got a phone call."

"And I told you that next time you'll help. Say, 'Yes, sir.' "

I never heard if Millie said "Yes, sir" again or not because the next thing I heard was, "*Papillon!*" and Malcolm and I were tumbling in the Orgone.

Tallulah says, "*A child actor is a vacuum that Nature has every right to abhor.*"

fourteen

MALCOLM AND I resumed walking to and from the school bus together, and Malcolm even sat up front behind the driver with me. One day, as Malcolm and I boarded the bus together, Lynette and the other clones started chanting, "Malcolm and Jeanmarie sitting in a tree, k-i-s-s-i-n-g . . ." I walked straight up to Lynette and very quietly but firmly said, "When my birthday is a national holiday, you're going to want to remind everyone that we went to the same school, so you just better stop what you're doing." She looked at the clone sitting next to her for support, but the clone was deliberately staring out of the window, so Lynette looked back at me and started to say something, but I shook my finger at her and said, "Don't do this to yourself," and she shut her mouth. Several days later she made a feeble attempt to tease me about my future fame, but

I put a stop to it by very quietly saying, "Careful, or I'll tell my biographer to leave you out." I could see that she began to think of me in a different way, and although some of the other clones warmed up toward me—especially whenever they were feeling on the outs with her—Lynette Hrivnak and I were never to become friends.

❧ ❧ ❧

TALLULAH approved of our plan to have everyone meet at Washington Square Park on Midwinter's Night. She said that once we found The Regina Stone and she had Then Spot potty trained her soul would have some rest. I told her that I didn't think she looked very restless, that she always seemed to be lounging about in her blue satin pajamas and never seemed to be anything but relaxed, and I would add a *very* to the kind of relaxed she seemed to be. Tallulah looked me over—top to toe, elbow to elbow—and said, "You forgot, darling, that Tallulah is an actress."

Tallulah was the only adult I had ever talked to who could be two things at once: herself and the equal of a sixth grader. Other adults couldn't. They always showed how proud they were of "being able to communicate with the child on her level." It was disgusting to listen to them. I always heard that paid-for, patient sound of a social worker talking to someone on welfare. None of them could stand up to five minutes of one-on-one with someone from middle school. In the days before Tallulah, I thought that adulthood was a secret club whose members were more concerned with keeping people out than letting them in. They seemed always to close a door behind them.

But not Tallulah. She opened doors. She was not always kind, and she had enough respect for Malcolm and me to allow herself to be irritating. She never pretended that what was important to us was important to her. Tallulah told us that she had little need to pretend. "After all, darlings, Tallulah has the stage for that."

At last I told Tallulah that I dreamed of becoming an actress. She was not surprised. "You must want it very much," she said matter-of-factly.

"I do."

"Wanting is not enough; you must also try. And try out."

"I may try out for a part in the spring play. They are going to do *Rumpelstiltskin*. I would like to play Rumpelstiltskin himself."

I explained how ever since I had first heard the story in grade school, I had felt that Rumpelstiltskin had been given a bum rap.

In the first place, only a very greedy person would promise someone her future baby in exchange for gold. In the second place, if the miller's daughter hadn't become queen—and she never would have without Rumpelstiltskin—she wouldn't have had hundreds, maybe thousands, of messengers to send out into the kingdom like a secret service to find out what Rumpelstiltskin's name was. If the miller's daughter had been investigated by Congress, she would have been indicted for using dirty tricks to get elected, for abusing power and for not giving the handicapped an equal opportunity. I thought the miller's daughter was a snot.

"Do you think Mrs. Spurling will agree with my interpretation of the part?" I asked.

"If she's brave, she will. I don't know this Mrs. Spurling.

155

I don't know if she will be ready to do the part that way. Timing is important. There is talent, of course. You've got to have the right stuff. But you must also have the right timing. The world must be ready for you when you are ready for it. Some people call it luck, and it is luck. Some people call it getting a break, and it is that, too, but I know that without it, you cannot be a star. If you are a painter or a composer, and your work has a life beyond your own, you can become a star after your death, but I must tell you, darling, death is greatly overrated as a maker of immortality."

Malcolm said, "I don't see how anyone can become immortal without first dying."

"Unfortunately, that is true. And isn't it a bore, darling?"

Malcolm said, "What about me? I don't want to be an actor. I want to be a scientist."

"You want to be a star scientist, don't you?"

"Yes, but what has that got to do with what you're saying."

"Listen to Tallulah, darling. She is about to be profound." Malcolm started to smile but quickly realized that Tallulah was not making a joke, so he listened, and Tallulah said, "There is no difference between being an artist and being a scientist."

Malcolm replied, "Yes there is. A scientist is methodical. A scientist thinks logically. A scientist uses algorithms."

"What is an algorithm, darling, some form of birth control?"

"No. It is a mechanical procedure in mathematics."

"Well, darling, a true scientist is not an algorithm. He is an artist, not a mechanic. Both are seekers of truth. The truth may be poetic in one case and factual in another, but if you are going to be merely logical and merely mechanical, you will never be a star. Just as an actress has to think as well as feel, a scientist must feel as well as think."

"That's only two," I said.

"What's only two?" Tallulah asked.

"Talent and timing. What's the third thing that it takes to make a star?"

"I'll let you find that out when you find The Regina Stone."

❦ ❦ ❦

ON ONE SINGLE DAY, three kids in my class came down with flu, so I gargled three times before coming to Rahab Station. Malcolm said that my breath smelled like a hospital corridor, and I told him that he could have gone the rest of his life without making that remark. My body scent must have changed, for Spots, Now and Then, sniffed me vigorously when I arrived at Rahab Station. Tallulah must have noticed, too, even though I had heard that people who smoke a lot lose their sense of smell. She told me that I worry too much about germs.

"You are really trying to protect—excuse the expression, darling—your internal organs against an attack. You want them to be perfect." She took a long drag on her cigarette and said, "Tallulah can tell you that they will get hurt anyway. And really they must. An unscarred performer is truly empty calories: sweet but not nourishing."

❦ ❦ ❦

EVERY DAY from the time that Malcolm and I made up until the Friday that school was dismissed for Christmas recess,

we went to Jericho Tel and found Now or Then Spot waiting, and we visited with Tallulah. She told wonderful stories
about the theater, and she always had something funny to
say. I remember many of the things she said, and because I
don't want to waste them, I have written them at the be-
ginnings of these chapters, the way that writers used to do
long ago.

The weeks from Thanksgiving to Midwinter's Day, the
last day of school for the year, flew by. We hardly noticed
that Tallulah had not sent us Topside since we had made
contact with Patrick Henry Mermelstein.

Tallulah says, *"If you must complain in public, either be amusing or outrageous."*

fifteen

MIDWINTER'S DAY opened with a cold, damp chill that made a person glad it was the shortest day of the year. After I got home from school, Mother called from the airport saying that there was so much air traffic that she had been asked to work another shift. I told her that I would be fine without her. At seven o'clock I bundled up and left the trailer, anxious to get to Jericho Tel. Malcolm was waiting for me by the steps of his trailer. He, too, was bundled up. He wore a stocking cap and a long striped scarf that he pulled up over his mouth. Neither one of us took a hand out of a pocket to wave. His father had also called to say that he had been asked to work another shift.

We walked fast and were at Jericho Tel by ten minutes past seven, and we began our wait. It was so cold that each minute felt like ten. Our bones seemed to conduct the cold straight up, so we stamped our feet and danced, trying to give the hard frozen ground less surface to chill. We took our hands out of our pockets only to look at our watches, which we took turns doing. When it was five minutes before eight, I began to suspect that Spot would not appear; at eight o'clock, I knew that we would not be called to Rahab Station. We waited five minutes more.

Malcolm complained, "I don't understand this at all. Tallulah approved of our plan to meet the buskers."

"We'll have to go to Washington Square by surface," I said.

"That will take hours."

"Then we'd better start now."

"Listen, Jeanmarie, I think we ought to go home and take a hot bath. Finding The Regina Stone is Tallulah's problem, not ours."

"Wrong. It's ours. If we don't find it, we'll never know the third thing that it takes to make a star."

Malcolm was stamping his feet up and down, doing the jittery dance that people waiting at a bus stop do on a cold day. He took a mittened hand out of his pocket and stretched it out toward me. "Come on," he said, "we'd better find a way to get to Washington Square."

We started running toward the exit of Empire Estates, thinking we would hitch a ride on the main road, when we saw Dapper Dan the Diaper Man toss a stack of soiled diapers into the back of his panel truck and walk around to the driver's side of the cab. "Hey!" Malcolm called. "Hey! Dapper Dan. Dapper Dan." He got his attention. "Are you heading back to the city?" he asked.

"I'm going home. Can you believe this? Eight o'clock on a Friday night, and I'm just finishing up. I'm driving through rain and sleet and dark of night out here, practically to the end of the island to make two rotten deliveries. Two. Two deliveries at the end of the world."

Malcolm asked him if he would let us ride with him as far as he went.

"I go as far as Westbury."

"We really need to get to Greenwich Village, but we'd appreciate a lift as far as you'll take us," I said.

We hopped into the front of the truck, and Dapper Dan introduced himself. "My name isn't Dan. It's Norman. Call me Norm." Then he began a long series of complaints about the diaper business and about his brother-in-law. "I just come out of the Army, and this brother-in-law of mine says, 'Listen, Norm,'—the family calls me Norm—this brother-in-law, he says to me, 'The babies are booming. You know what's the choicest gift people can give at a baby shower?' 'What?' I ask like a dummy. 'A gift certificate for the services of none other than yours truly, Dapper Dan the Diaper Man. One week, two weeks of a gift certificate, and you have these mothers hooked. They don't never want to wash no dirty diapers. Ever.' It makes sense to me. He lets me look at the books. I see the figures. The business looks good. So I buy it. Wham, bang, my brother-in-law, he's out of the business and retired down in Florida, sending me post cards.

"I buy all these huge washing machines and all these commercial dryers to say nothing of thousands of dozens of diapers. You've got your newborns, your prefolds, your five-ply crotch for night. I am practically a department store of dia-

161

pers. What my dear brother-in-law neglects to tell me is that with the baby boom comes the home appliance boom, and every little mother wants her own darling's tushy wrapped in his own private diapers. When I explain that I sterilize all the diapers, they don't listen. They talk like they are a branch office of General Hospital.

"I tell you, now that it is too late, I see that rock bottom is just a little downhill from here. Paper. It's coming. Mark my words, paper diapers are on their way, and those few mothers who can't get to a washing machine are going to be papering their babies' behinds, and I am going to be stuck with tons of commercial washers and dryers and a department store of diapers. I used to be a gift certificate. I used to be smiled at and invited in for coffee. Now, all they do is leave the soiled on the back step. I never see anyone. They pay by credit card. I take VISA, American Express, Diner's Club."

Neither Malcolm nor I said much. Norm did all the talking, and before we knew it, he was watching the highway exits to turn off for Westbury. I said, "Norm, would you consider taking us into Greenwich Village if Malcolm gives you an idea about how you can turn your fortunes around?"

Norm saw Malcolm give me a mean look. "Who you fooling?" he asked.

"I'm not fooling anyone." I turned to Malcolm and said, "It's all right if you give Norman your idea, Malcolm."

Malcolm said, "I don't know what you're talking about, Jeanmarie."

"Don't pretend, Malcolm. You know that you can save Norm's business." Malcolm pinched my arm and made mean faces. "I know you promised your aunt that you wouldn't tell anyone, but I think that Norm here deserves a chance. It's all right if you tell him."

Malcolm relaxed and smiled. "I expected to get something more than a free ride into the city for my idea," he said.

"But he has all the equipment, Malcolm. Your aunt doesn't."

Malcolm muttered under his breath but loud enough for Norman to hear, "If my aunt finds out that I've given away my idea, she'll probably write me out of her will."

Norm said, "Am I supposed to believe that you got an aunt that's got a will?" He said, "The next exit for Westbury is coming up." He glanced nervously at Malcolm and then checked his rearview mirror and changed lanes. "Heck, I haven't been in the city in a long time." He drove along in silence for a while and then asked, "Where did you guys say you needed to go?"

We told him Greenwich Village. "Hey, I'm glad you told me. I can't leave a couple of nice kids like you alone in the Village on such a cold night. That place is Weirdsville, I tell you. They got more freaks per square mile down there than Barnum and Bailey."

We said very little for the rest of the way. When we were almost out of the Midtown Tunnel, Malcolm said to me, "That's city lights at the end of the tunnel. Glad." He smiled. I smiled back.

Norm asked, "What was that? What d'ya say, kid?"

I said, "We were just reviewing history."

"History?" Norm said. "For my money, history just keeps on happening."

163

WHEN WE GOT to Manhattan, Norm drove straight down Fifth Avenue, and Washington Square loomed up in front of us. I was excited, anxious to get out and find the buskers. I asked him to let us out. He had to circle around before he could pull over to one of the side streets and park. Malcolm reached across me and started to open the door. "Wait a minute, kid," Norm said. "You said you have an idea for my business. Time to tell."

Malcolm said, "Blue jeans."

Norm said, "What about them?"

Malcolm said, "The thing I hate most about new jeans is having to break them in. I only like them after they've been washed about ten times. I know I'm not the only person in this world who hates to break in new jeans. So I think that what you ought to do, is to contact the people who manufacture them and tell them that you will give them a good softening in your commercial washing machines. That way, they not only will be pre-softened, they'll also be pre-shrunk."

I said, "At Singer Grove it's considered low fashion to wear new blue jeans."

Norm said to his steering wheel, "You know, sometimes, you gotta obey your instincts." He patted the steering wheel with both hands. "Yep," he said, "something told me that I should pick up you two kids. And something else told me that I should listen to what you might have to say. I like your idea, kid. I like it a lot."

Malcolm said, "I also think you ought to put pebbles in the washers to soften the denim. That way you can call it 'stone-washed.' Better to make them *be* soft and *sound* tough."

"Right," Norm said. "Good idea. Stone-washed. I like it. I really like it. *Stone-washed*. Listen, kids, I haven't bummed around the Village in a long time. I don't mind having a night out on the town. How about I come with you, we buy you a bite to eat, and I take you back. Who knows, you might come up with one more good idea." Malcolm told him no, thanks, that we had business to do. "Sure," Norm said. "I understand. I can understand that." But I knew he was disappointed that we hadn't asked him to join us.

Tallulah says, "*If ever you want to learn the difference between accuracy and truth, look at a photograph of Gertrude Stein and then look at Picasso's portrait of her.*"

sixteen

IT WAS AFTER ten when we got to Washington Square. There were not many people waiting around. Those who remained were gathered around a mime with a painted white face who was bumping into imaginary walls. Malcolm and I hurried through the crowd looking for familiar faces. We saw none. We broke up. He circled left, and I circled right, and we once again made the rounds of the crowd. No success. I said, "Either we missed them, or they did not show up." At that moment we were both looking up Fifth Avenue, and we saw a woman wearing a long skirt and an old-fashioned cape walking between two men. There was no mistaking who they were, and Malcolm and I started to run to catch up with them.

They were walking, skipping and hopping, three abreast, up Fifth Avenue with their arms woven around each other.

Every now and then we heard their laughter like metal wind chimes on a cold, almost still night. They stopped often to hug each other, and a fresh wave of laughter would tunnel down the street. Malcolm and I were within a half a block of them when they turned and entered a restaurant.

We quickly made our way there and walked in. We were immediately met by a woman in a long black skirt who told us that unaccompanied minors were not allowed in. Rules had not been something that we had had to worry about when we had been invisible. I told the woman that Malcolm and I were accompanied and that we had just temporarily become separated from our accompanists. "Please tell the trio with the dummy that Tallulah's friends have arrived."

"I'm terribly sorry," she said, "but you can hardly expect me to know which of my customers is a dummy."

"Would you please page Mr. Simonescu?"

She became downright snippy. "This is not an airport; it is a high-class establishment. We have no paging system. You two just better run along now."

"Do you think I could make up a name like Simonescu?" I asked. "Nicolai Ion Simonescu. Please call him."

"Does he have a reservation?" she asked. I told her that he did not. Then she said that she had no way of knowing where he was, no way to call him, and that we better run along.

She didn't say in which direction we were to run along, so Malcolm and I bolted into the restaurant just in time to see Nick, P.H. and Emmagene sitting down in a booth in a far corner. "Hey, Nick," I called, and all three of them looked around. Nicolai started to get up from his seat, but the hostess signaled a waiter to come help her. The waiter

167

pinned Malcolm's arms behind his back, and the hostess squeezed me into a bear hug, but she had not covered my mouth, and I managed to yell, "Tallulah sent us. Tallulah, Nick. Tallulah." Nick lifted himself from his seat but still hesitated. "You!" I yelled. "Yes, you, Nicolai Ion Simonescu. We want to see you." Nicolai looked puzzled, but he stood up and came over and told the hostess and the waiter to let us go.

"We're here about Tallulah," I said.

"Where is she?"

"All around," I said as the hostess let me go, and the waiter let Malcolm loose. I immediately linked one arm through Nick's and the other through Malcolm's and headed toward the corner booth.

Malcolm and I sat down. My breath was coming in razor slices that were whipping my throat. I asked for a glass of water, and Emmagene pushed hers toward me. I drank the whole glassful, and Malcolm drank Patrick Henry's. They didn't take their eyes off of us. Nick asked if we would like more water and pushed his goblet in my direction, but I shook my head no. "Then," he said, "it's time for you to tell us what is happening?"

"Where's Anna Karenina?" I asked.

"Under Emmagene's cape."

"She must be suffocating," I said.

"In all the excitement, I almost forgot about her," Emmagene said, smiling but doing nothing toward rescuing Anna Karenina.

Nicolai said, "I don't understand what is going on, but come, let's make room for Anna Karenina."

Malcolm and I were seated side by side along the wall,

and we inched apart and made space for Anna Karenina; only then did Emmagene pull her out from under her cape. "It all seems so strange," she said, "that the three of us should happen to meet after all these years, and that the name of Tallulah should come up. It doesn't seem to make much sense."

"Or it all seems to make too much sense," P.H. said. He studied Malcolm. "Say NOW HEAR THIS, NOW HEAR THIS."

Malcolm said it, trying to make his voice lower than it really was. Patrick Henry cocked his head and listened. "Have you ever been to The Magic Flute in Elmhurst?"

"Is that a restaurant?" Malcolm asked.

Patrick Henry said, "I have the strange feeling that I have heard this voice before, and I have the stranger feeling that I have lost all control of this conversation. Would someone mind telling me what is happening? Or if that information is not available, would someone mind telling me who you are?" We introduced ourselves, and when Patrick Henry heard Malcolm's last name, he said to Nicolai and Emmagene. "I don't think our meeting here is one hundred percent coincidental."

After P.H. said that, I asked Emmagene if she wouldn't like to remove her cape. She said that she would prefer leaving it on, that she got awfully cold and always took a long time to warm up.

The waiter interrupted to take our orders, and as he did so, Emmagene withdrew a notebook from under her cape and began to write. She sighed and closed the book. "How many songs have you left to sing?" I asked.

"Five hundred and forty-two," she answered, not at all surprised that I would know what she was writing. But Nick and P.H. looked puzzled, and I enjoyed being mysterious. Then for the first time ever, my visible self took control of an adult conversation. I felt like the conductor of a symphony; I could lift a baton and make the violins play; or I could wave my hand and make the drums roll, but all I did was to ask questions quietly and calmly.

"We're going to play catch-up," I said. "First, Emmagene."

She smiled bashfully. "There's not much for me to tell. I'm pretty much the same as I was when I last saw Nick and P.H."

"Why don't you start by telling us about how you got your break."

Her sigh was deep enough to lift her shoulders. "There's not even very much to tell about that, unfortunately."

"Did you really perform in that night club in the Village?" Nicolai asked. "I heard that you did."

Emmagene studied her gloves. She took them off and began pulling at the fingers, straightening them out, one by one. "A coffee house," she said. She continued to study the gloves as she answered, "About ten years ago, I was singing outside Carnegie Hall, and a man came up to me and said, 'Young lady, it has been years since I have heard a voice as sweet and pure as yours. You should be singing inside Carnegie Hall, not outside on the sidewalk.' He gave me his card and told me he ran a coffee house here in the Village, and that he would feature me for his Saturday night show."

"Wow!" Patrick Henry said. "That was always a dream of mine."

"What happened?" Nick asked.

"Nothing really. I sang my songs. The audience applauded, and I left the stage. The next Saturday the same thing, and the next. I performed there for six weeks, but nothing happened. No one reviewed my show. No one who came seemed to tell any of their friends about me. I didn't catch on, so I went back out on the streets."

"Did that man give you your break before or after Tallulah died?" I asked.

In a motion so rapid that only someone reading body language would notice, Emmagene's hand flew to her throat. She cleared her throat and lowered her eyes. "After."

The waiter brought our orders, and during the silence that followed, while everyone started eating, I picked up Anna Karenina and began speaking through her to Emmagene.

ANNA: Tell me, Emmagene, how you like my new cape what Nicolai made for me for this reunion occasion.

EMMAGENE: [*Smiling.*] Oh, I like it very much, Anna.

ANNA: I like vairy much your cape. But is vairy hot now in this place. Anna will now take off her cape and show to you her beautiful shoulders.

EMMAGENE: You are very vain, Anna. You always were.

ANNA: Why you not also remove your cape?

EMMAGENE: You won't see any beautiful shoulders. You will see only some old clothes.

ANNA: And maybe something else.

EMMAGENE: Yes. Moth holes.

ANNA: No, I think that what else we will see is something vairy interesting.

There fell a silence over the table, as if someone had suddenly sucked all the air out of our corner of the room. "Take off your cape, Emmagene," I said.

She undid the clasp and let her cape drop over the back of the chair. Beneath the cape was a down-filled jacket that was rubbed slick at the elbows.

"Take off the coat, Emmagene."

She slowly undid the toggle buttons. P.H. reached his arm over the back of her chair and helped her pull first one arm and then the other out of the sleeves. He took the coat and laid it over his lap. Beneath the coat appeared a gray wool turtleneck sweater that was worn thin at the elbows and that had one frayed cuff and a moth hole near the shoulder.

"Take off your sweater," I said.

She didn't do it right away. We locked eyes across the table, but I had had good practice at stare-downs, and I did not flinch. She furrowed her brow and looked to P.H. and to Nick for support, but they sensed that more than Emmagene was being uncovered, so they avoided returning her look. She pulled the sweater over her head, and Nick took it from her, folded it and put it to one side of the table. Beneath the sweater was a high-necked calico pinafore made with a half a hundred hand-sewn tucks. This time, no one needed to ask, and Emmagene offered her back to Nick, and he undid the buttons. I looked over at Malcolm to see if he would be embarrassed, but he was not. After all the buttons down to her waist were undone, Emmagene turned around and looked at each of us in turn. She looked at Nick for a long, long time, and her eyes filled with tears. Her lips formed the words, "I'm sorry," and she dropped the straps

of her pinafore. There, at the pulse point of her throat spark-
led the diamond that had once belonged to Tallulah.

For a long time no one said anything. Maybe Nick needed
a minute to realize what it was. Malcolm and I needed
time to realize that our quest was over. At last Patrick Henry
said, "It's The Regina Stone, isn't it?"

Emmagene nodded.

Then Nicolai asked, "Why?" He repeated asking why,
asking himself as much as Emmagene.

"I needed it," Emmagene said. "It was Tallulah's lucky
piece. Her talisman, she called it. I thought that if I had it,
I would get my break."

"And you did," Nicolai said.

"I did, and I didn't," she answered.

P.H. said, "You did. You got your break, Emmagene. You
had talent. What more did you need?"

"The third thing," I said.

"The third thing," Malcolm repeated. "She didn't have
the third thing." He picked up Emmagene's book. I nodded.
"It's in the book, isn't it, Jeanmarie?" I said, yes it was. Malcolm flipped the pages back to the dates when she was singing in the club. He read, "March 3, '*Greensleeves*,' '*Mary's
Hill*,' '*Shenandoah*'; fifteen thousand, one hundred twenty
eight songs left to sing." He read a few more entries: fourteen thousand six hundred and twelve songs left to sing . . .
eleven thousand one hundred and six songs left . . . He
flipped through the pages until he was at the end. "December twenty-second: '*Scarlet Ribbons*,' '*London Pride*'; five
hundred and forty-two songs left to sing." He closed the
book and handed it back to her. "You've written your own
account of why you'll never be a star."

Emmagene took the book from Malcolm and opened it. "Where is it written that I shall not be a star?" she cried. Her hand went to the necklace at her throat. "Where does it say that?"

"It's written on every page, Emmagene," I said.

"I still don't understand. I am not a greedy person," she said. "Nick," she said, her eyes filling with tears, "you know I'm not greedy, don't you?"

He smiled and nodded. "I know you're not, Emmagene."

Malcolm said, "The book is not saying that you're greedy, Emmagene. It is saying that you are not generous. You never have been. You are not generous with your talent. You keep track, you have always kept track, and you shouldn't."

We looked at Nick and P.H. and knew that they understood, too. Even with a lucky break, a person like Emmagene could never be a star. Not because she had no talent but because she had talent and was stingy with it. Stars can't hold back. Emmagene had only eighteen thousand songs to sing, and she kept track. Stars can't be afraid of letting go. Stars must be willing to expose themselves. I said to Malcolm, "We found what Tallulah wanted us to find."

Emmagene reached up and started unfastening the necklace. "Don't," I said. "Keep it. You have only five hundred and forty-two songs left, Emmagene, and then you will need to live off what The Regina Stone can bring you. Keep it."

Emmagene slid her arms back into her pinafore and turned her back so that Nick could fasten the buttons. She took her sweater from his lap and pulled it over her head, and then Patrick Henry helped her into her coat; she stuffed her gloves into her pockets. Nick got up and tenderly placed her cape over her shoulders. She cradled the book in her arms and stood by the side of the table. "I'm leaving now," she said. "I just don't understand. I took the necklace for luck. Do you believe me, P.H.?"

Patrick Henry looked sad. "I believe you, Emmagene."

Emmagene looked again at the book, her eyes brimming with tears. "I simply do not understand." She stood there with her cape half falling off of one shoulder, shaking her head and repeating, "I don't understand." She looked at Malcolm and me—most especially at me—and said, "You still have all your songs left to sing, you can afford to be generous."

"If I'm to be a star, I can't afford not to be," I answered.

Emmagene left the room without a single backward glance.

We remained sitting at the table. The waiter reappeared and asked if he could bring us dessert. Nicolai nodded to the waiter and asked us if we wanted anything else. Malcolm said, "A ride home."

Tallulah says, "*A happy person strikes a balance between doing good and doing well.*"

seventeen

MALCOLM AND I went to Jericho Tel early the next day and the next, but Spot, Now and Then, never appeared.

We were worried that Tallulah was annoyed with us because we had not returned with The Regina Stone. We wanted to explain why we had allowed Emmagene to keep it, and we wanted to hear from her that we had done right.

I tried to make bargains with history. If Tallulah would ask us back, I would: clean up my room and never again argue with Mother; be not just nice but extremely nice to Lynette Hrivnak as soon as school started; give up pizza for three months. I pledged all my Christmas money to the United Fund, wished on the first star I saw at night, didn't step on a crack or walk under a ladder or spill salt, but we didn't find Spot waiting at Jericho Tel.

Malcolm's aunt and uncle in Elmhurst invited Mother and me to Christmas dinner at their house. We went.

I didn't know if the Soos were friendly or if they were just uncritical, but Mother and I felt at home, and it seemed natural that we would volunteer to help with the dishes. After dinner and dishes, we all assembled in their living room to exchange presents. I gave Malcolm a western leather belt with a genuine brass buckle that I had ordered from a store in Texas, and he gave me a book, *A Parliament of Sounds: Poems to Read Out Loud.*

Malcolm asked Millie to do some tricks. She said that she was surprised that he was interested. "Lose some; win some," he said as he looked at me and smiled. I knew what magic we had lost, and as good as Millie was, she was not a patch on being invisible.

After Millie finished, Malcolm picked a bulb off the Christmas tree and held it under his chin like a microphone. "And now," he said, "coming to you directly from the Empire Estates Mobile Homes Park, is Jeanmarie Troxell, who will read to us from her new book." He handed me the book, opened to Ogden Nash's poem, "The Carnival of the Animals." At a signal from him, Reuben put a record on; I recognized it as the one he had played at The Magic Flute when Malcolm had interrupted. As the music played, I read the poem. I was not perfect, but I was wonderful.

And *it* was wonderful.

Performing was wonderful. It was a lot like being invisible: the outside Jeanmarie disappeared altogether.

I made up my mind that I would try out for a part in the school play.

$$\mathscr{y} \mathscr{y} \mathscr{y}$$

Tryouts were the first Friday we were back. I was nervous doing it, but I read for the part of Rumpelstiltskin. I was the only girl who did. I certainly didn't want to be the miller's daughter. Late on Saturday Mrs. Spurling called me at home and told me that I had the part.

I looked at the new calendar on our refrigerator door. It was January 6, Twelfth-Night. I called Malcolm and told him. He came over, and we lit candles and sat at the kitchen table and talked about Tallulah. We knew then that we would never see her again.

When Malcolm left, I circled the date of my first play.

I knew I would make mistakes, but I knew I would be wonderful.

And I did.

And I was.